NANTUCKET THREADS

PAMELA M. KELLEY

PIPING PLOVER PRESS

NANTUCKET THREADS

Izzy's life is about to change soon in the biggest way possible. She is excited and nervous and torn about whether or not to give her ex, Rick Savage another chance. Rick has tried to be a better man. He's gone through anger management classes and really seems to be making an effort. But is that enough? Does she owe it to him, to them, to try one more time? Or is it okay for her to move on and possibly even consider a future with someone else? Not that she is looking to do that, but there is someone else who she has known as a friend for a long time. He's a very good friend and at times she wonders if there could be something more there. But, she has bigger things to consider first. Someone other than herself and it's all new to her. But, her sister Mia is there to help. Izzy is now living with Mia since her condo was renovated. And Mia has a promising new romance. And there's a lot going on with the Hodges family too. Kate has a very big announcement and Lisa learns that she has been violating a major rule for her bed and breakfast. So changes are coming....

CHAPTER 1

"Mom, I have some happy news." Kate paused to make sure she had her mother's full attention and something in her voice gave Lisa goosebumps. Instantly she knew what her daughter was about to say and her heart filled with joy.

"Are you..." Before she could finish the sentence, Kate jumped in happily.

"Yes! Jack and I are expecting a baby. You're the first to know."

Lisa smiled as she remembered the conversation from a month ago. She glanced at the soft baby sweaters on the seat next to her. She'd bought them in town the day before and couldn't wait to give them to her daughter.

"Earth to Lisa..." Sue said with amusement. Lisa stopped daydreaming and snapped her attention back to her two best friends, Sue and Paige, who were visiting for Saturday morning breakfast. Her daughters, Kristen and Abby, were there too, and Abby's daughter Natalie, who was napping in her stroller. Normally her oldest, Kate, would be there as well, but she and Jack were off in the Cayman Islands on their honeymoon. They were due back the next day. They were originally supposed to go right after their wedding, but a nor'easter in Boston put that plan on hold and they rescheduled for a month later.

"Sorry, I spaced for a minute. What did you ask?"

"I asked if Kate knew what she's having yet," Paige said.

"No, not yet. She has an appointment scheduled for next week, and I think she might find out then. She's a little over four months along now. That's why I got this cute sweater set in both pale blue and in powder pink." She held up the baby sweaters and matching pants. They were so tiny and she couldn't wait to see the baby in them. Everyone oohed and aahed as she passed the sweaters around the table

"How is Kate feeling?" Sue asked.

"She's been lucky so far. She hasn't really had any morning sickness, which is why she didn't realize right away that she was pregnant. She's always had an irregular cycle too, so didn't think much of it that she was running late."

"I'd say she's very lucky," Abby agreed. "My first trimester was not fun."

"Good that she's feeling well and can enjoy the Cayman Islands. Have any of you been? I did a cruise years ago that stopped there for a day, and I've always wanted to go back. It's just beautiful. The water is so clear and clean. I'd rather be there right now," Paige added as she glanced out the window.

Lisa followed her gaze and saw snow blowing and whipping through the trees. She could almost feel the cold just by looking outside. She hoped that Kate and Jack were having a good time and enjoying their break from the winter weather.

"Are you girls ready for the big storm that's coming this weekend?" Lisa asked her daughters. Another nor'easter, a snowstorm with heavy winds that had a good chance of knocking power out, was predicted for that Friday, followed by two more days of snow.

Abby made a face. "I'm sick of winter already. And no. I need to go to Stop and Shop when I leave here and stock up on a few things. I need batteries too, and maybe another flashlight."

"I'm in good shape," Kristen said. "I'll probably go hunker down at Tyler's. He just had a delivery of wood for his new stove, so even if the power goes out, we'll be nice and warm. And he's a decent cook too."

"Good thing they are coming home tomorrow," Sue said. "They say it's going to be the only sunny day this week."

Lisa was grateful for that too. She was always nervous when her kids were traveling, and she wouldn't be able to fully relax until Kate and Jack were back home on Nantucket.

"There's a sale on rotisserie chickens at the market. I

picked up two yesterday. I got a bunch of snack foods too, in case we lose power. And we're well stocked with wine, of course." Paige grinned. Her boyfriend Peter Bradford owned a liquor store, and that's where they all bought most of their wines.

"Did you have many cancellations for this week, Mom?" Kristen asked.

Lisa nodded. "Yes, everyone has either cancelled or rescheduled. Except for one lady, Marley Higgins. She's still planning to arrive tomorrow and is staying for a month. So, that will help make up for the cancellations." Normally the dining room would be filled with guests helping themselves to the breakfast that Lisa always set out—usually a quiche of some kind, plus fresh fruit, bagels and toast. But today it was just her family and friends.

"A month? This time of year. That's interesting. What do you know about her?" Sue asked.

"Not much. Just that she's traveling alone and she asked for a list of my favorite restaurants, which I was happy to help her with. If we get snowed in, we can take her food for lunch and dinner if need be. Hopefully, it won't be too bad though. It could still change direction and go out to sea."

"Let's hope," Abby agreed and then changed the subject. "I ran into Izzy yesterday. Natalie and I were walking around downtown and I popped into her store. She has some really cute new things, and she's started to carry more shoes too. I was tempted, but then remembered I'm a mom that doesn't need fancy shoes."

"You can always use a good pair of shoes. Just because you're a mother doesn't mean you can't look nice and get out now and then," Kristen reminded her.

Abby smiled. "You're right. Maybe I'll drop back in soon. There was a really cute pair of red boots that I might need another look at."

"How is Izzy doing? Is she starting to show yet?" Lisa asked. Izzy's sister Mia had stayed at the inn while her condo was being restored after a fire, and Lisa had grown fond of both girls.

Abby shook her head. "No, not really. She's so tiny anyway and she was wearing leggings and an oversized sweater. So, if there is a baby bump, I couldn't see it."

"She must be close to five months along, by now?" Kristen guessed.

"I think so. Her stomach will probably pop a little in the next few weeks, I bet," Abby said. "She looked great. Her skin was glowing and her hair is so long and really healthy. My hair looked great when I was pregnant too," she added wistfully.

Lisa laughed. "Your hair always looks good, honey."

"She's not back with her ex, I hope?" Kristen asked.

"No. I don't think so. I didn't ask though. She mentioned that she's still staying with her sister, so hopefully that won't change once she has the baby. I know he was pushing for her to move back in with him, but like I said, we didn't talk about it. She asked after all of you though and said to say 'hello'."

CHAPTER 2

"So, what do you think? Is it a crazy idea?" Izzy took a deep breath and waited for her sister Mia to say something. It was a lazy Sunday afternoon, and they were relaxing in Mia's recently renovated waterfront condo. Izzy still couldn't believe what a wonderful job their friend Will had done with the restoration. The hardwood floors gleamed and the new rugs and fresh paint on the walls made it all feel like new. You'd never know there had been a fire.

Mia's fluffy white Pomeranian, Penny, was curled up between the two of them, as they sat in the living room, on the very comfy cream-colored sofa, sipping hot chocolate and sharing a big bowl of heavily buttered popcorn. The Hallmark channel was on and they had about ten minutes before the next Christmas movie would begin. Even though it was well after the holidays, they still loved their Christmas movies. Izzy liked the feeling of warmth and hope that they gave her, especially as her own world was a bit unsettled.

Mia took a sip of hot chocolate before setting the mug down and turning her attention to Izzy. "You want to expand the store and go online. That sounds like a big project, and an expensive one. Are you sure you want to take that on, now?"

Izzy knew that her big sister, who was only a few years older, was just worried and being protective. Even more so since Izzy was five months pregnant by her now ex-boyfriend, Rick Savage, who Mia was most definitely not a fan of. But Izzy had thought this through and weighed the pros and cons for several weeks. The small clothing store that she'd worked at and then bought from the owner when she retired was a labor of love. Izzy had studied fashion in college, then worked in a management training program at Macy's in Manhattan before vaca-tioning with her sister one summer on Nantucket and stepping foot into the Nantucket Threads shop.

She and the owner, Faye, had got to chatting and clicked immediately, and Faye had offered Izzy a job on the spot. Izzy's parents, who thought the Upper East Side of Manhattan was the only place in the world to live, worried that their daughter was giving up a tremendous opportunity with Macy's. But Izzy knew in her gut that it was the right thing, and she'd never regretted it once.

Izzy only sold things that she loved in her shop and she seemed to have a good feel for what others would love too. She carried an assortment of touristy hats and sweatshirts, most with the word Nantucket printed or embroidered across the front. Those were her biggest sellers by far, especially in the summer. But every year, sales of her other clothing items and carefully curated shoe collection grew.

She nodded. "I'm sure. I researched this pretty carefully. I think if I expand and take over the shop next door, and add the online store, I should be able to double my income and possibly my profits eventually too. Once the initial startup investment is paid off."

"Do you need a loan for that? They are not always welcoming when you are self-employed."

Izzy grinned. "No kidding. And especially a single mother-to-be. I'm not sure I'd be keen to loan money to me, either. But I'm not looking for a loan. I have some money saved. But, before I do this, I wanted to also make sure you are really okay with me staying here after the baby comes? I know you offered, but it's a lot to ask."

"It's not at all. You're family, Izzy. And I'm going to be an Aunt for the first time. I can't wait to meet my new niece or nephew. There's plenty of room here and you're the best roommate—the only roommate I'd consider having now."

Izzy breathed a sigh of relief. "Good. I feel the same way and that gives me some breathing room to get the store expansion up and going and successful. We should be out of your hair hopefully in a year or so."

Mia reached for the bowl of popcorn. "So, tell me more about your plans, and how the online store will work. I don't think many of the shops on Nantucket have an online presence, do they? Are you sure it's worthwhile?"

Izzy leaned forward, excited to share her ideas.

"Well, the shop next to mine is smaller, about half the size, so I won't be doubling my rent. Just going up by about half, so it's not too much, I don't think. It will give me room to expand and try new things—maybe have a few more shoes, for example, as those have been going over well."

"What about the online store? How would that work?"

"I'm actually really excited about having an ecommerce site. I can partner with vendors that will handle the shipping and fulfillment, so I don't have to deal with that or have a big warehouse. I can still ship some custom orders myself too. I already do that a little now even without a website, as you know."

"Right. I know customers just call and ask you to ship things and you always do it."

Izzy laughed. "Of course I do. That keeps them coming back. And a sale is a sale. One of them recently said something interesting, though. She loved one of my sweatshirts and when her sister saw it on her, she wanted one, too. But they couldn't find anything similar online at all. That's when she called and asked me to mail one off. But it got me thinking... Some of my designs are really unique and popular, and if I can drive traffic to them online, I might be able to sell them anywhere."

"Who will you have do the construction work? It shouldn't be that much, just knocking down part of the connecting wall? It's a small job, but maybe Chase Hodges can do it or know of someone you could call."

Izzy smiled. "Will actually said he could do it."

Mia looked surprised. "Really? You already talked to him about it? I thought he mostly did restoration work and furniture building these days."

"He does, and he's really busy. But, he stopped in the store this week when he was downtown and we got to chatting. I ran the idea by him and he offered to do the work. Insisted, actually. He said it shouldn't take him more than an afternoon or two and he could do it over a weekend."

"That's nice of him. So, he thinks it's a good idea too?"

Izzy knew that Mia respected Will's opinion. Will was a good friend to both of them and while he didn't know the retail business, he knew building and construction and he'd lived on Nantucket longer than either of them.

"He does. He said every year, traffic and the overall economy on Nantucket grows. And it's too good of an opportunity, with the shop next to mine coming available. He said it would be crazy not to do it."

Mia laughed. "Well, that settles it then. For what it's worth, I agree. I'm just naturally more cautious. But, you've done a great job with that shop. I'm sure it will be a success."

"Thanks. I think it will be. I'm excited about it."

Izzy's phone buzzed, and she glanced at the caller ID and saw that it was Rick. She knew why he was calling. He wanted to meet. To talk her into getting back together. They'd broken up and soon after, she'd learned she was pregnant. Rick had never wanted to break up and when she told him about the baby, he swore he'd do better and begged her for another chance. She'd said no at first, but when he went through an anger management program and seemed to be really serious about changing, she agreed that they'd talk after the holidays.

"Hi Rick."

"Izzy. How are you? I've missed you."

"I'm good. How are you?" They'd spoken briefly the week before when he'd called to wish her a Merry Christmas. He'd wanted to set a date for them to meet then, but she'd suggested they catch up after the holidays.

"Better than ever. The new job is going good. I think this one is going to stick." Rick's anger issues had spilled over into his work as an electrician, and he'd been let go from his previous two jobs after just a few months.

"That's great, Rick. I'm glad to hear it."

"So, do you want to get together this Thursday after work? We could go to Millie's, get some tacos and talk." Rick knew Millie's was one of Izzy's favorite restaurants. It was casual, on the beach, and had the best Mexican food on the island.

"Sure. That works for me."

"Great, see you there at six."

Izzy ended the call and saw the concern in Mia's eyes.

"You're going out to dinner with Rick? Are you sure that's a good idea?"

Izzy sighed. "No. But I agreed weeks ago to meet him after the holidays, to talk. I think it's only fair to hear what he has to say."

"Hmm. Well, you know how I feel about that. Be careful, Izzy."

CHAPTER 3

Kate finally relaxed when she glanced out the window of the small plane and saw Nantucket straight ahead. The sight of the island always calmed her. It had been a wonderful trip, but she was happy to be almost home. She caught her husband Jack's eyes as she settled back in her chair. He gave her hand a squeeze, and she sensed he was thinking the same thing. Jack was even more of a homebody than she was. They'd both been born and brought up on Nantucket, but Kate had left for a while, for college and then to work at a magazine in Boston.

Though, like many of those who left the island, Kate found her way back eventually. It seemed like almost another lifetime since she'd lived in Boston. And now she couldn't imagine living anywhere other than Nantucket again. Everyone she cared about was there. Her friends, her family, and Jack. And soon their new family member would arrive.

"Do you think you're ready to dive back into your story, now that we're back?" Jack asked.

Kate was a full-time mystery writer now. And while she loved writing mysteries and knew it was what she was meant to do—it didn't always go smoothly. There were lots of fits and starts when she'd hit bumps along the way and just get stuck, not sure where the story needed to go next. She'd hit one of those bumps in a big way before the honeymoon and decided to leave her laptop at home and take a full week off from writing, something she hadn't done since she moved home.

But it was what her mind needed. She found that she got some of her best story ideas when she wasn't writing but was instead doing something completely unrelated, like driving or taking a shower. Or relaxing on a Cayman Islands beach and snorkeling. The snorkeling had been amazing. And one afternoon while they were on a harbor cruise and Jack was drinking a rum punch and she was sipping fruit juice, she stared through the boat's clear glass floor at the sea creatures swimming below and her mind unlocked, sending a rush of ideas.

When she got back to the hotel room that day, she jotted some of them down, so she wouldn't forget. She was excited about her story again, and eager to open her laptop and get going.

"Yes, I'm ready. More than ready. Especially if the storm is as bad as Mom said it might be. We could be snowed in with no TV or internet...nothing to do but write."

Jack laughed. "Hopefully it won't be that bad. Or if it is, it won't be out for long."

"I'm just glad to be home. I don't mind if we get a storm and have to hunker down a bit. It will be fun."

"I don't know if fun is the word I'd use," Jack said as the small plane smoothly touched down on the runway of the Nantucket airport. "But it is good to be home."

Once they landed and found their luggage they called an Uber, which quickly arrived and fifteen minutes later, they walked through their front door. Kate realized that traveling all day had caught up with her and she was utterly exhausted. She yawned as she slowly made her way into the kitchen. Jack grabbed her suitcase along with his and brought them into their bedroom, while Kate heated up some water for a cup of tea. She thought it might wake her up a bit as she was suddenly struggling to keep her eyes open.

Jack came into the kitchen and watched her closely for a moment.

"Why don't you go take a nap? You look like you're about to fall over. Do you feel okay?" She could hear the worry in his voice.

"I'm fine. I just might take a short nap, though. After I have my tea."

"Take as long as you need. I'm going to run to the store and stock up on a few things. I think we need batteries for the flashlights and I'll grab some snack stuff in case we lose power."

"Okay. Thanks, honey. I'll see you when you get

back." Jack left and Kate took her cup of tea into her bedroom. She changed into her most comfy sweats and crawled into bed. After having a few sips of tea, she snuggled into her pillow and a moment later was out cold.

CHAPTER 4

"Marley, please join me." Lisa smiled at her only guest, who had just filled her plate with a slice of spinach and artichoke quiche and some fresh cantaloupe and was glancing around the empty dining room. Marley had arrived the night before, exhausted from a long day of traveling. Lisa had welcomed her, settled her into her room and made sure she knew to come for breakfast the next day.

Marley smiled as she settled into the seat across from Lisa.

"I hope you slept okay last night?" Lisa asked as she lifted her coffee mug.

"Like a log. They cancelled the fast ferry reservation I'd initially booked because the winds were too strong, and I wasn't sure when they'd reopen. But they died down thankfully and I only had to wait a little over an hour."

"You're lucky. Sometimes they just shut totally and people are stuck until the next day. I'm glad you made it."

Lisa was curious to know more about Marley. It was unusual for someone to stay for a month, especially in the middle of winter. She guessed that the other woman was about her age, mid-fifties and noticed that she wasn't wearing a wedding ring.

"I'm glad too. I would have just gotten a hotel by the ferry, there are several along the water. But I was anxious to get here and get settled. Especially as I hear there is another storm coming this weekend."

Lisa nodded. "It might be a big one, with high winds that could knock out the power. That might put a damper on getting into town and going to restaurants. But we have a full-house generator here, so if the power goes out we should be fine for several days—and it rarely stays out longer than that."

"Oh, that's good to know. I'm going to head into town soon to stock up on some snacks and soups, things I can heat up in my room."

"If we're snowed in, we'll make sure you have plenty of food. You won't go hungry here," Lisa assured her.

Marley smiled. "Thank you. Have you lived here very long?"

"Over thirty years now." Lisa told her about her four children and her new husband, Rhett.

"He was my first guest here. I tease him that he is the guest that never left. But we both feel very blessed."

Marley nodded and was quiet for a moment. She took a sip of coffee and a bite of quiche before speaking again.

"My divorce was finalized a little over a month ago.

Frank and I were married for almost thirty years and have two children, both in their late twenties. Sophie lives in Los Angeles and is a production assistant for a sitcom. My son Nate is a software engineer at a startup in Silicon Valley. Frank and I owned a business together in San Jose, a retail e-commerce site. Maybe you've heard of it—The Attic?"

Lisa was impressed. "Yes, of course. My girls love The Attic. They've bought some gorgeous pillows and throws from there, and clothes too, I think?"

"Yes. We started that business together. It was Frank's idea, but I helped and learned a lot. We grew apart over the years and had different ideas on what we wanted The Attic to focus on. Ultimately Frank felt like it was his baby, so I allowed him to buy me out." She smiled sadly. "So, I suppose I'm retired. But I feel too young to retire." She sounded a bit adrift and Lisa's heart went out to her.

"You're definitely too young to retire, but I imagine there are all kinds of interesting things you could do now. Possibly start another business?"

"Maybe. It has crossed my mind. I just don't know what the right thing would be. I am going to take some time off. Just relax and see if any ideas come to me."

"That's smart. What brings you to Nantucket? Especially this time of year? I love it here in the winter, when it's quiet and peaceful, but most people prefer the summer months which are more lively."

"We used to vacation here, when the kids were young. We both had normal jobs then. Once we started The Attic, it kind of took over our lives and it was impossible to take more than a day or two off to go anywhere, especially clear across the country to Nantucket. Now that the divorce is final and there's nowhere I have to be, I thought it might be nice to get away. I thought I could get a feel for what it would be like this time of year if I stayed for a month or so. To see if I could see myself staying for longer than a vacation."

"That's a wonderful idea. I think it's good to spend time somewhere before buying a place. You can see how you like it, and if you enjoy the solitude of our winter. Even if you buy a place though, you could always just come for the summer if you find it too quiet this time of year. Many people do that." Lisa had always thought it was a shame that so many beautiful homes on Nantucket sat empty for the better part of the year, but it was very common.

"There's another reason I decided to come here too." A mischievous gleam came into Marley's eyes and Lisa leaned forward, curious to hear her reason.

"So, it's kind of silly, but my birthday was about six weeks ago, and my daughter got me a psychic reading. I don't usually put much stock in those kinds of things, but they are fun."

"They are. My girls love that too. Kate once had a group of us over one night for a tarot card reading. What did yours say?"

"Well, it was a lot of what you'd expect. Sometimes the readings are so general they could apply to almost anyone. She talked about new beginnings and letting go of the past. But then she got very specific and said she saw me traveling to an island on the east coast. I asked if she meant for a vacation and she shook her head and said it felt like it might be more permanent than that."

"And that's when you decided to book a trip here?" Lisa asked.

Marley shook her head. "No, not yet. It planted the idea, but I was still feeling kind of stuck and not ready to go anywhere or do anything yet. It wasn't until my friend Audrey had a night like your daughter Kate. She invited a bunch of her girlfriends over for cocktails and had a tarot reader that was recommended as the 'best' and he gave each of us a reading."

"Was it similar to the other one?"

"You could say that." Marley laughed. "But he was even more specific, and said, 'I see you in a big house — it's white or light gray. I see the ocean in front of it and a ferry in the distance. I think it's Nantucket. Have you ever been there? I was stunned of course and just nodded. He was quiet for a moment and then looked into my eyes intently and said it was important that I go as soon as possible."

"Did he see you moving to Nantucket?" Lisa was intrigued by Marley's story.

"He didn't say. Just that it was important for me to come here and that I would find what I need. Whatever that means. I was shaken and still hesitant, but Audrey convinced me to come. She searched online and found the Beach Plum Cove Inn, and here I am."

"Well, I'm glad you're here. And I hope your visit is a

good one. You'll see a side of Nantucket that most people never see."

"I'm looking forward to the peace and calm." A moment later, she added, "I thought I might teach myself how to knit. It's something I've always wanted to try and never made time for. I noticed there's a yarn shop downtown. I thought I might stop there today, too."

"That's a great idea. And the owner, Eloise, has beginner classes in the shop on either Monday or Tuesday mornings. You might enjoy that."

"I might. Thank you." Marley took the last sip of her coffee and stood. "It's been lovely chatting with you. I think I am going to venture off and explore a bit."

"Have fun. Please let me know if you need anything." Lisa smiled as Rhett walked into the room and decided to have a second cup of coffee with him before heading into town herself to run some errands.

CHAPTER 5

Izzy changed outfits several times before settling on what felt like the right thing to wear to meet Rick. She didn't want to look like she was making too much of an effort, but she still wanted to look nice and she couldn't understand why she was feeling butterflies at the thought of seeing him in person. Her feelings for Rick were complicated and she couldn't just turn them off completely.

She twirled and checked her appearance in the mirror. The pale blue long cashmere sweater was one of her favorites and flattered her long, wavy blonde hair. She wore her pregnancy jeans, the ones with the soft elastic front that was much more comfortable over her growing stomach. She knew that most people wouldn't have any idea that she was pregnant, as she didn't have a baby bump yet, just a thickening that, so far, she was able to easily hide with long sweaters. But her regular jeans were too tight around the waist now.

She added a swipe of pink lip gloss and ran a brush through her hair, smoothing out her flyaway curls. She'd been taking pregnancy vitamins and her hair had never looked so good. It was glossy and thick, and the curls behaved better. For the first time, she stopped wishing for her sister's straight hair.

Penny jumped off the sofa and ran to her when Izzy walked into the living room. Mia was due home any moment, but Penny's wagging tail meant she was ready for a walk.

"Come on, let's go." Izzy clipped on Penny's harness, grabbed hold of her leash and they set out for a quick walk around the boat basin, the marina area where Mia's condo overlooked the harbor. They walked down along the wharf, which was quiet. Most of the boats were tucked away in storage for the winter, so there were few people out and about.

As they walked, Izzy thought about her relationship with Rick. They'd met at the Club Car, a popular restaurant downtown. Izzy had gone there to meet Mia for after-work drinks on a Friday. But Mia had called just as Izzy walked through the door. She was in a meeting with a particularly demanding and fussy bride and was going to be delayed for at least a half hour. She felt terrible, but Izzy had told her not to worry. Izzy was perfectly capable of having a drink by herself at the bar.

So, she'd ordered a glass of chardonnay and sipped it slowly, while she relaxed and people-watched from her bar seat. It was a summer night, and the Club Car was busy with tourists and the usual end-of-week, Friday night crowd. Izzy noticed a few familiar faces—people she knew were locals from seeing them around town.

So when Rick had walked over and took the seat next to her, she recognized him as a year-round resident, from seeing him driving his truck with the ladder in the back. She figured he did something in construction. He smiled when he asked if the seat was available, and since she knew Mia wasn't going to be there for at least a half hour, she'd simply nodded. He'd said he was waiting for his friends too and they got to chatting. The spark between them had been electric and immediate. So when Rick asked if she wanted to go out sometime, she didn't hesitate.

It was fast and intense with them from the beginning. Izzy had never been so physically attracted to someone. When Rick looked her way, it was like his dark eyes saw through to her soul. Mia had been a little worried that they'd gotten serious so fast and regretted that she'd been late that day. Izzy might never have met Rick if she'd been on time. But Izzy knew that everything happened for a reason.

Life with Rick had been wonderful at first, and she'd moved in with him after just a few months, which Mia had never thought was a good idea. But by that point, they were both in love. And at first, it had been exciting, but the honeymoon phase soon wore off as Rick grew more comfortable with their relationship and she began to see a side of him that she didn't like quite as much.

Rick didn't have a lot of patience and he was quick-tempered, moody and unpredictable. Izzy thought she'd seen him at his worst though, and he was always apologetic after they'd fought. He'd never been violent towards her, not really. Just the one time he grabbed her arm to try to get her to leave a party because he was jealous that she was talking to her friend Will.

She knew he'd been under a lot of stress and it had carried into his work. He'd lost two jobs due to losing his temper. But he'd managed to hold on to his most recent job, which came through a friend. And when Izzy had had enough and ended things, Rick finally realized that he had a problem.

He enrolled in an anger management course, a twelve-week program, when he discovered she was pregnant. She'd dreaded telling him, because she knew he'd try to talk her into getting back together. And he had tried. He'd never wanted to end things. He swore that he was a changed man, that the anger management course had helped. She hoped that was true, for his sake. But she didn't think it was a good idea for her to try again with him. She doubted that he could change so much that it would make a difference. But she needed to hear what he had to say. He'd wanted to meet sooner, but she'd pushed him off until after the holidays.

It grew darker as she and Penny walked, and colder. After about ten minutes, they were both ready to go home. And a quick glance at her phone told her it was time to leave for Millie's.

About twelve minutes later, Izzy pulled into the parking lot at Millie's restaurant, which was on the other side of the island, by the beach. Rick's truck was already there. She went inside and upstairs to the bar and found Rick sitting at a high-top table, drinking a beer that was still full. So, he'd arrived just a few minutes earlier. He stood when he saw her and smiled, and her heart skipped a beat.

Rick's smile with those craggy laugh lines around the corners of his mouth and eyes still had a powerful, physical effect on her. His smile reached his eyes and she could see that he was genuinely glad to see her and was also a bit nervous. She seldom saw the vulnerable side of Rick. He was usually pretty sure of himself, but things between them were uncertain at best. He pulled her in for a hug.

"It's great to see you. You look amazing." His glance fell on her stomach. "You wouldn't even know," he added as Izzy slid onto her chair.

"I think you'll be able to tell very soon. This sweater hides the fact that I no longer have a waist. It's gone, completely. I can't button my jeans anymore."

Rick raised his eyebrows. "You have jeans on now and look as skinny as ever."

She laughed. "These are not my regular jeans. They have an expandable waist. Which is a good thing, because I'm hungry and plan to order two different kinds of tacos."

"Excellent. You're feeling okay then? No morning sickness?"

"I've had some, but it's mostly eased off and now I'm in the hungry phase."

She looked up as a waiter arrived with a basket of chips, guacamole and salsa.

"I ordered the guac for you," Rick said.

Izzy appreciated the gesture. He knew she always ordered it and she was ready to dive in.

"Can I get you something to drink?" the waiter asked.

Izzy saw another waiter walk by with a tray of freshly made frozen margaritas. They looked delicious.

"Could I please get a virgin raspberry margarita?"

"Of course."

He returned a few minutes later with the frosty, non-alcoholic beverage and they put their orders in. Scallop and bacon, and shrimp tacos for Izzy, and a shredded beef chimichanga for Rick.

Izzy reached for a chip and dunked it in the creamy guacamole.

"So, work is going well?" she asked him.

Rick nodded. "Really well. Dave's a good guy and business is booming for him, so I've been able to work some overtime too, almost every week."

"That's great." His friend, Dave, owned the company where Rick worked and if this job didn't work out, Izzy didn't know where he'd be able to get a job. So she was glad, for his sake, that it was going well.

"How are things at the shop?" Rick asked.

"Good. Well, slow. It's always slow this time of year, of course."

"Have you thought of closing for the rest of the winter? You could move back in with me and you wouldn't have to work. You could relax and just take care of the baby when it comes."

"That's a generous offer." Izzy chose her words carefully. She knew Rick's goal was to get her back and for them to be a couple again and a family. But she wasn't ready to go there. Not yet, and maybe not ever. "I can't really afford to take the winter off, though on some days it is tempting."

She took a sip of her margarita, which was delicious but really not the same without the tequila. It was too sweet.

"I'm actually planning to expand the shop. I'm taking over the space next to me as that tenant is closing her business, and I'm going to start a website too and put the shop online."

Rick frowned. "Are you sure you want to do that? It sounds risky and expensive. Did the bank approve a loan?"

She shook her head. "I'm not getting a loan. I have savings. I've looked into this pretty carefully, and I think it will be a good investment. A way for me to grow my business and diversify, which should actually be safer in the long run."

"Hmm. I thought you were going to put that money towards a down payment on a house?" He didn't add the words that she knew he was thinking—our house. They'd once talked about buying a house together, when they'd also assumed that they would marry. Izzy would have happily put most of her savings into buying that house. But things were different now, and it felt like putting it into her business instead was the better investment.

"This feels like the right thing. Mia has said I can stay with her for as long as I like after the baby comes. I don't want to wear out my welcome, but it's nice to have that option and I'm thinking a year at most. If my calculations and projections are right, I should be well on my way to replacing those savings by then."

Rick was quiet for a moment as he ate a few chips and took a sip of his beer.

"The course worked, Izzy. I've got a handle on my temper now. Things are good at work. I won't disappoint you again. I still love you and I think maybe you still love me too? Would you consider giving me another chance? For our sake and for the baby? We could be a family." He smiled and his eyes locked onto hers and she saw the hope there and the love. He really wanted this. He reached for her hand and gave it a gentle squeeze. "I've missed you, so much."

When Izzy stayed silent, her emotions warring within her, he released her hand and simply said, "Please just say you'll consider it? We can take things slow, ease back into it, go on a few dates. Whatever you want, Izzy."

Izzy let out the breath she hadn't realized she was holding. "I'll think about it," she said finally.

Their waiter arrived with their food and they dove in and the conversation turned to less serious things. Rick told her about the project he was working on and what some of their mutual friends were up to, and she filled him in on how things were going with Mia and Sam. She found herself enjoying their time together. Rick could be funny and she'd forgotten that side of him. He was definitely more relaxed now, and he really seemed sincere. He was trying.

So, when they finished their meal and the check came, Rick insisted on paying. And when he walked her to her car, gave her a respectful hug and asked if they could meet again soon for dinner, she said yes. It felt like the right thing to do, and it was just dinner.

MIA LOOKED UP WHEN IZZY WALKED INTO THE CONDO. She and Penny were in their usual spots on the living room sofa, watching TV. Izzy took a breath, readying herself for Mia's questions. She didn't have to wait long. She'd just removed her shoes and settled on the opposite side of the sofa, when Mia spoke.

"So, how did it go? Did you tell him it's over for good?"

"Not exactly. We actually had a nice time. Rick seems good, really good. Like the Rick I first met."

Mia didn't look happy to hear it. "Please tell me you didn't agree to see him again? I'm sure he still wants to get back together and have you move in again? Did you tell him you're staying here after the baby comes?" Her sister fired the questions at her.

"He does want to get back together, but we knew that. I didn't agree to anything other than dinner. I said I'd go to dinner with him next week. I don't see the harm in that. Even if we're not still together, we can be friends. That's important, for the baby's sake."

Mia looked disappointed and skeptical. "Friends. Do you think Rick is capable of that? Are you right now?

You look all starry-eyed, Izzy. Don't trust your hormones."

Izzy laughed. "It's not hormones. I loved him once. It's not easy to just turn that off. Especially when he's trying. Really trying. People can change."

"I suppose anything is possible. But, I just worry about you Izzy. I don't want to see you hurt again."

"I know you don't. I don't want to be hurt again either. But you have to trust me to do what feels best for me and for the baby. Like I said earlier, it's just dinner."

"Well, you know how I feel. I'm here for you, whatever you decide."

"Thank you, Mia. I really don't think you have anything to worry about."

Izzy's phone dinged, and she glanced at the text message and smiled. It was Rick.

"How about next Saturday night at The Gaslight for dinner and some music? There's a good band going to be there."

Izzy typed back, *"Sure, sounds good. Talk soon."*

She looked up and Mia's eyebrows were raised. "Is that him already? Kind of fast, don't you think?"

But Izzy shook her head. "I think it's sweet, actually. There's a good band next weekend at The Gaslight. Rick knows I love hearing live music there. It was one of our favorite spots."

"Sam and I like it there too. Maybe we'll join you?" Mia suggested.

Izzy hesitated for a moment, then nodded. "Great. I'll let Rick know. I'm sure he won't mind." She wasn't actually sure of that, but she thought it might be interesting to see how Rick behaved around Mia and Sam. There had always been some tension there as Mia had never really approved of Rick, and Izzy was pretty sure that Rick sensed it. If he was able to stay calm around Mia and have a good night, that would be a good test of how much he really had benefitted from the anger management course.

CHAPTER 6

The wind was already howling Friday morning when Kate stepped outside onto the front step to get the morning newspaper. The air was so cold and damp that it went right through her. She hurriedly grabbed the paper and shut the door tightly behind her. The big storm, the nor'easter everyone had been talking about all week, wasn't due until later that evening.

The wind was always stronger by the ocean, though. Jack had already left for work and Kate poured herself a second cup of black coffee and brought the paper into the office where her laptop was firing up. She wasn't ready to dive into the writing just yet, though. Some days, most days, she had to ease into it. She had a morning routine where she drank her coffee, read the news headlines and then stared out at the ocean, waiting for inspiration to strike.

She noticed as she sipped her coffee that the waves

were already looking frothy, bigger than usual and with white caps. The trees by the house were swaying. But there was no rain or snow yet. Just the promise of what was coming. She finished reading the paper, then set it aside and opened Scrivener, the software program she wrote her first drafts in. She read over what she'd written the day before, made a few tweaks and then began her work for the day.

Nearly two hours later, she jumped when her cell phone rang, startling her. It was Jack.

"Hey, just checking in with you. It was pretty windy when I left today. I think we might close up a little early today, around four or so. We'll play it by ear. How's the writing going?"

Kate laughed. "It was going great until I almost jumped out of my chair when the phone rang."

"Oops. Sorry about that. I'll let you get back to it... feel like some fish for dinner? I could bring home some haddock for us."

"I actually have some short ribs I thought I'd cook up. My mom's recipe. Does that sound okay?" Kate was in the mood for comfort food.

"That sounds amazing. Call me if you need anything."

"I will." Kate smiled as she ended the call. Jack had grown very protective of her since she discovered she was pregnant. He checked in on her at least once, sometimes twice a day when they were slow at the store. They never talked for more than a few minutes, but she liked the connection, especially as she spent most of her day alone.

Writing was a solitary job. Sometimes, for a change of scenery, she'd bring her laptop downtown and settle in for a few hours at one of the many coffee shops. There were always others doing the same thing, now that so many people worked remotely.

She stood to stretch her legs and use the bathroom. As she walked, she suddenly felt strange, like something wasn't right. A crampy feeling that she hadn't had in months made her a little concerned as she reached the bathroom. Another wave of cramps, a bit worse this time came, and she was really alarmed when she saw some light bleeding in the toilet.

Her first instinct was to call her mother, who, after having four children, would know what might be going on and what she should do. She answered on the first ring and Kate told her how she was feeling.

"Do you think it might be a miscarriage?" Kate asked as another cramp came.

"Oh, honey, I hope not. It's probably nothing. Sometimes there's light spotting. I had that once or twice. But call your doctor. You have an appointment on Monday anyway, right? Maybe they can squeeze you in today if you tell them what's going on? Call them and call me back. If they can see you today, I'll drive you over."

Kate appreciated that. She didn't want to pull Jack out of work and, while she could have driven herself, she would happily let her mother do it. She looked up the doctor's phone number, called and breathed a sigh of relief when they said they could see her in an hour.

Kate called her mother back and also called Jack to let him know.

"I can come take you," he said immediately.

"Jack, it's probably nothing, hopefully. My mother's not busy and she wants to drive me over."

"Okay. But call me as soon as you know something."

"I will."

Kate watched the clock after that. Her concentration was gone, and she wasn't able to do any more writing. She was concerned that the cramps were still coming. And there was more blood when she used the restroom shortly before her mother came. It seemed like more than light spotting to Kate, but she really didn't know what to think. Her pregnancy had gone so smoothly so far and they were looking forward to the ultrasound on Monday to learn what they were having. She'd had her first ultrasound at barely eight weeks when she first suspected she was pregnant, and it was too early to see much at that point.

She heard her mother's car pull into the driveway and grabbed her coat and purse and hat and gloves. She didn't usually bother with the hat and gloves, but it was too cold not to today. She slid into the passenger side of her mother's Volvo station wagon and her mother smiled brightly.

"Okay, we're off. I'm so glad they could squeeze you in, honey. It will be okay, you'll see," she assured her. But Kate could see the worry in her eyes, too.

The wind had died down a little, but the air was still heavy and calm. So calm that it was a bit eerie. The streets were mostly deserted, as very few people were out and about unless they had to be.

A few minutes later, they pulled into the parking lot of the doctor's office. Kate and her mother made their way inside. The waiting room was empty and the receptionist, Caroline, smiled when she saw them.

"Thank you so much for getting me in today," Kate said.

"It worked out well as we had two cancellations, people wanting to reschedule because of the coming storm, right before you called. The doctor will be right with you."

They took a seat and two minutes later, the doctor's assistant came to get her.

Kate followed her into an examination room and she checked Kate's vitals—blood pressure, weight and temperature—before leaving and said the doctor would be in shortly. Kate changed into a paper Johnny and waited.

A moment later there was a knock and Dr. Leslie Johnson entered the room. She was very direct but also warm and friendly, and Kate felt very comfortable with her.

"Kate, good to see you. Tell me what's going on?"

Kate filled her in and she nodded. "Okay, let's take a look. There are a few possibilities. How are you feeling right now?"

Kate realized she was feeling a bit better. "The cramping has slowed down, actually. I feel okay right now."

"Good. Scooch down to the end of the table and put your feet in the stirrups. I'll take a look inside and then we'll do a quick ultrasound."

Kate did as instructed and a few minutes later, the doctor told her she could relax and take her feet out of the stirrups. She squirted some warm gel on Kate's stomach and slowly ran the ultrasound wand all around her stomach, stopping now and then to check the image on the screen. Kate glanced at the screen, but it all looked like a blur, a slightly moving blur. Finally, the doctor stopped and handed Kate a cloth towel to wipe the gel off her stomach.

"Okay, I have some good news and some not-so-good news. The not so good news is you have a common condition placenta previa which is when your cervix gets blocked by your placenta and that causes the cramping and bleeding. It means that you need to take it easy and we have to keep an eye on you. But the good news is your baby is fine. Actually, your babies are fine." The doctor smiled. "You're having twins, Kate. It looks like a boy and a girl. Do they run in your family?"

"Twins? Really? Yes, I'm a twin. Are you sure?"

The doctor laughed. "Yes. Very sure. Look." She pointed to the monitor and the ultrasound image. "See, there are two babies here. We didn't see it when you first came in because you were so newly pregnant and it wasn't obvious."

Kate was feeling overwhelmed and wished that Jack had come with her to hear this news. It didn't seem real. "Can I get a print-out of that ultrasound?"

"Of course. Congratulations, Kate. Why don't we see you back here in four weeks? And if you have any concerns, or cramping again, give me a call. Try to rest as much as possible, eat well, and avoid stress."

Kate nodded and agreed, feeling relieved but dazed by the news of twins.

Her mother stood as soon as she walked into the lobby.

"Is everything okay?" she asked anxiously.

"Yes. Have you ever heard of placenta previa?"

"That's something to do with the cervix, right?"

"Yes, the placenta blocks it and that's what causes the bleeding. I have to take it easy and come back in a month. She did an ultrasound, so I know if it's a boy or a girl now." Kate couldn't resist having a little fun.

"So, which is it?"

"Both! One of each."

Her mother looked confused at first, then thrilled. "Twins?! Kate, that's fabulous news." She laughed. "And perfect. I saw the cutest sweater set while you were gone and couldn't decide which color to get, so I got both."

"I can't wait to tell Jack. It's exciting, but a little scary too. Can I handle having two babies at once?" The thought of it seemed a little overwhelming.

"You'll be fine. The first year you'll be a little sleep-deprived." Her mother chuckled. "Okay, maybe a lot sleep-deprived, but it will go by fast and it's still a magical year. It will get easier after that. Especially once they are a few years old and have each other to play with. An only child is more demanding on your time."

"I do like the thought of not being pregnant again. One of each and we're done," Kate said.

"That's what we thought too, that we might just have you two girls. But then your brother and sister came along. You never know."

"That's true. I have to call Jack. He's going to be shocked."

CHAPTER 7

Izzy sipped her favorite afternoon treat, an iced decaf hazelnut coffee with a splash of chocolate syrup as she sat behind the register in her shop. Her laptop was in front of her. The store was completely empty, and she hadn't had a customer in over an hour. It was almost one thirty and the wind was picking up, rattling the front door now and then. All the ferries had already been cancelled, which meant the usual steady foot traffic along the wharf wasn't happening.

Izzy still had plenty to do though with planning the online store and she had been busy on the laptop all morning. But she could just as easily do that from Mia's condo. She'd been thinking of closing early anyway, by three at the latest, but maybe sooner could work too. She stood and was about to go flip the open sign in the window to closed, when a woman walked into the store. Izzy sat back down and smiled.

"Welcome to Nantucket Threads. How is it out

there?" The woman looked to be in her mid-fifties. She had a stylish shiny brown bob that reached her chin and was wearing a red wool hat and coat, and her cheeks were rosy.

"That wind is picking up! I wanted to walk down the wharf and check out the harbor before heading home, and I noticed your shop. The name got my attention."

"Thank you. Are you on vacation?" It was a strange time of year for it, but something about the way the woman spoke made Izzy think she was just visiting.

"Yes, you could say that. My family used to come here every summer when my kids were little. Then we all got too busy, life got in the way. I'm from California. It's a bit colder here than I'm used to."

"You're getting a real taste of our weather today. It's going to get bad later, possibly a nor'easter. I'm hoping the power doesn't go out, but there's a good chance it will." Izzy loved a good storm, as long as the electricity stayed on.

"I don't mind, actually. I've never experienced a big winter storm, and the place I'm staying at has a generator."

"Lucky you. I wish we did. Are you looking for anything in particular?" Usually when people came into the store, they were just wandering in and wanting to browse, but now and then someone was after something specific.

"Not really. I thought I'd just take a look around. These sweatshirts are lovely. This is a very pretty shade." She held up a pinkish-red sweatshirt to check the size.

"That's our most popular color. It's called Nantucket Red."

"I love it. If I'm going to be a proper tourist, I should get a Nantucket sweatshirt. I'll take it." She set it on the counter and then made her way around the rest of the store, looking closely at some of the sweaters and shoes. A few minutes later, she came back to the register with a pair of black fleece sweatpants and fluffy pink socks.

"I'm going for comfort, especially if we're going to be snowed in for a few days."

"That's smart. I live in sweats. As soon as I get home tonight, the jeans will come off and the sweats go on," Izzy said as she rang everything up, then wrapped it all in tissue and carefully placed everything in one of her signature pink and silver paper bags.

"You have some really lovely things here," the woman said. "I'll have to come back again when I have more time to poke around. I'm sure you're ready to close up soon."

"It's been very quiet today. I probably will close earlier than I'd planned."

The woman nodded and took the bag that Izzy held out to her. She glanced over at Izzy's shoe collection. "Have those black boots been selling well for you? We couldn't keep them in stock. They were flying off the shelves."

Izzy was intrigued. The boots the woman mentioned were a new item for her, and they had been more popular than she'd anticipated.

"Yes. I already placed a second order. Do you run a shop too?"

"Not anymore. I did. My ex-husband and I had an online business, The Attic."

"The Attic. The one that sells home goods too?" Izzy doubted it was the same one. The one she was thinking of was a huge national brand.

The woman smiled. "Yes, that's the one. We started it almost thirty years ago, first as a shop in San Jose and then things really took off when we went online." She held out her hand, "I'm Marley. Marley Higgins." As soon as she said her name, Izzy recognized it. She'd read about Marley and her husband Frank over the years and had admired the retail business they'd built.

She shook Marley's hand and introduced herself. "Izzy Maxwell. It's so nice to meet you. I'm actually just about to expand online myself. I'm taking over the space next door and building an e-commerce site." She laughed. "I don't really know what I'm doing with the online stuff, but I'm trying to learn, and I think it might be a good opportunity for growth."

Marley's eyes lit up. "Oh, it definitely would. I might have a few suggestions for you. And I could let you know a few mistakes we made, so you can avoid them. I could stop back in one day next week, when the weather is better, if you like?"

"Really? I would love that. That would be so amazing. Maybe I could hire you, as a consultant? I don't want to take up your time while you're on vacation." Izzy was excited about the chance to run her ideas by Marley.

Marley laughed. "I'm here for a full month with all

the time in the world. Tell you what, you can buy me a cup of coffee. How's that? And we can chat a bit."

"Thank you. I really appreciate it. Here's my card, call or just stop in whenever it's convenient for you."

Marley took the card and tucked it in her purse.

"It was nice meeting you, Izzy. I'm off. You should do the same soon, too."

"I will." Marley opened the door to leave and a rush of wind blew in and Izzy shivered. The temperature felt like it had dropped at least ten degrees and the cold went right through her. Marley was right. It was time to close up and go home.

———

AS SHE WAS MAKING HER WAY HOME, WALKING THE SHORT distance from her shop to Mia's condo on the wharf, she noticed a familiar truck pull into the small supermarket straight ahead. The driver smiled and waved her over. It was her good friend Will. She walked over and he got out of the truck.

"I thought that was you. I'm running into the store for batteries. Thought I had some at home. Are you and Mia all set for the storm?"

Izzy nodded. "We stocked up on everything earlier in the week." She grinned. "I picked up more wine yesterday, so we're ready now. She and Mia were looking forward to making a nice dinner and relaxing while the storm howled outside. "We're hoping the power stays on," she added.

"It doesn't sound good. I have a generator at my place though, so if it stays out and you guys want to crash with me any time over the weekend, I'll come get you. Just give me a call."

"Thanks, Will. We should be good, hopefully."

"Well, if it gets too cold, just give me a holler."

A huge gust of wind whipped through Izzy's hair and she shivered. "Will do. Bye, Will. It's too cold out here for me!"

CHAPTER 8

Kate added the last splash of red wine to the big cast-iron pot on the stove and gave the short ribs a stir. She'd browned them first with some garlic, carrots and onions and then added mustard, spices and a full bottle of cabernet. The alcohol would all burn off as it cooked, and it already smelled amazing. She covered the pot and put it in the oven. It would simmer for a few hours until the meat fell off the bone. By the time Jack got home, it would be ready, and she'd make a side of fluffy whipped potatoes and some steamed broccoli. It was one of her favorite comfort food meals, and Jack's too — perfect for the weather.

It wasn't snowing yet, but the winds were getting loud and the waves on the ocean had grown, looking like an angry swirl of whitecaps as they raced toward the beach and crashed on the shore. Kate made herself a cup of tea, grabbed two chocolate chip cookies she'd made the day before and took it all into her office, where she could stare at the ocean and think about what needed to happen next in her story.

She eventually figured it out and was startled a few hours later when the front door opened. She glanced at the time. Jack was home about an hour earlier than expected. It was snowing now, coming down fast and furious. She was glad that he'd decided to leave work early. She closed her laptop and went out to the kitchen to say hello. She didn't see him right away but a moment later, he was back holding a big plastic container of ice melt, little pebbles of salt that he would sprinkle on the steps and front walkway so they wouldn't go flying when everything froze up.

"How is it out there?" Kate asked.

"It's getting bad fast. Roads are already slick. We shut things down early. No one was coming in."

"I'm glad you're home. I have short ribs in the oven. Should be ready in about an hour."

"They smell incredible. How are you feeling?" Jack pulled her in for a quick kiss. "I still can't believe we're having twins. I don't think it's sunk in yet." Kate had called him as she and her mother were leaving the doctor's office earlier that day, and he'd been equally excited and shocked. She understood exactly how he felt.

"I'm good, totally fine. Taking it easy. I've just been puttering around the kitchen this afternoon and writing."

Jack smiled. "Glad to hear it. I'm going to head out and spread this stuff around. I'll jump in the shower after that."

"I'm going to head back into my writing cave for a bit."

Kate worked on her story for another forty-five minutes before shutting the laptop down and heading into the kitchen to check on dinner. She could tell by the smell that the short ribs were ready. She pulled them out of the oven and poked at one of them with a fork, and the meat shredded easily. She put the lid back on to keep everything hot and got the potatoes and broccoli that she'd made earlier out of the fridge and put them into the oven to warm up.

A moment later, she jumped as a wind gust sent a tree branch whipping against the kitchen window. It was a soft branch, so it was just a scraping, but showed how strong the winds were. Five minutes later, the lights flickered twice then went out for about ten seconds before coming back with a whirring sound and Kate knew that meant the generator that Jack had installed a few months ago had kicked on. She'd questioned if they really needed it at the time, as the power didn't go out all that often on Nantucket. But Jack had always wanted one, and now she was glad they had it. She glanced out the window and saw that the streetlights were out and houses across the street were totally dark.

Jack was in the shower—she could hear the water running. She called her mother and sisters, curious if they'd lost power too. Abby and Kristen still had it, but they both lived a little further inland, where the wind was slightly less wild. Her mother answered on the first ring and beat her to the question.

"Did you lose power, honey?"

"We did. But now we know Jack's generator works."

"Good! Ours just went out too, but we should be good for a few days. Hopefully it will come back on sooner than that. It usually does. How are you feeling?"

"I'm fine. At least now I know why I've been so hungry." Kate had never had a weight problem before. She enjoyed food like the rest of her family, but she'd never been a big eater.

"Take advantage of it, honey. Enjoy it while you can."

Kate laughed. "Oh, I am. I made short ribs. Used your recipe."

"That sounds good. I've been cooking this afternoon too. Baked a big loaf of sourdough bread and I have a tray of lasagna in the oven. We'll be eating that for the next few days."

"How's your new guest? I don't know that I'd be too happy about going on vacation and being stuck in a nor'easter."

"I don't think she minds. She wants to see what it's really like living on Nantucket in the winter. Better to find out now before she decides to buy property here."

"True. But I wouldn't want to be stuck in my room all weekend. She's not going to be able to drive anywhere for at least a few days. Jack said the roads are terrible and getting worse."

"I saw her at breakfast today and she was heading into town to do some shopping. She said she was all set with soup for tonight, but when I see her at breakfast tomorrow, I'm going to insist that she join us for dinner.

Maybe we'll play some cards or watch a movie. She seems very nice. Did you know she and her husband owned that website you girls like so much, The Attic? Well, her ex-husband owns it now. That's how she can afford to buy something here."

"No, you didn't mention that. She sounds interesting. I love The Attic. I actually just bought a cute pillow for the baby's room last week. That reminds me, I should probably go buy another one. I need two of everything now!"

"Yes, you do. Have I mentioned how excited I am that you're having twins?"

Kate laughed. "Maybe once or twice."

"Okay, I'll let you go, honey. Enjoy your short ribs."

Kate ended the call and was still smiling when Jack walked into the room, his hair still damp and looking comfy in sweats and a sweatshirt. "Was that your mother?"

She nodded. "They lost power too. Not yet for Abby and Kristen. Are you hungry?"

"Starving, actually." Jack poured water for both of them while Kate made their plates and brought them to the table. They chatted easily over dinner. Kate told him about her mother's semi-famous guest.

"Cool. I've heard of The Attic, but have never seen the site. Just the commercials. I don't do as much online shopping as you and your sisters. That reminds me, though—speaking of your mother, I meant to tell you something yesterday and it slipped my mind."

"Tell me what?"

"Well, I don't know if there's anything to it, but I overheard something I probably wasn't supposed to hear. Two ladies in line for seafood were chatting, and they mentioned your mother. I don't think they made the connection that I'm married to her daughter. Anyway, I recognized one of them—she owns another bed-and-breakfast and she said something strange like 'Lisa Hodges should have known better. She's going to be in a lot of trouble now.' And they seemed quite pleased about that. Any idea what they might be talking about?"

Kate frowned. "Violet? She was a bit of a trouble-maker when my mother was trying to get town approval for the Beach Plum Cove Inn. I have no idea what she was talking about. My mother hasn't mentioned anything."

"Well, maybe don't say anything then. No sense getting her upset. Hopefully there's nothing to it."

CHAPTER 9

Lisa was up early the next morning. She glanced out the kitchen window at her backyard and the ocean beyond. It was all a blanket of white and, for the moment, the snow had stopped. Normally, even in the cold weather, she'd go for her walk along the beach, but not today. She had no interest in trudging along in what looked like four or five inches of snow.

So instead, she decided to try a new recipe. Usually, she made a quiche of some sort or scrambled eggs and bacon along with fresh cut fruit and bagels, muffins and toast. She thought it might be fun to try to replicate her favorite breakfast dish from Panera. There wasn't one on Nantucket, but now and then when she was on the Cape, she'd stop into the Panera in Hyannis. She loved their breakfast puff pastry that was filled with a cheesy hot custard.

She made hers in a muffin tin, pressing store-bought puff pastry in the cups and baking that first, then pouring in the spinach, cheddar and artichoke custard and baking until it was set and the pastry golden. She hoped that Marley was in the mood for something a bit decadent. If not, Lisa would be eating them for the next few days.

When the pastries were done, she brought them into the dining room and set them on a warming tray. Then added fresh fruit, muffins and bagels just in case Marley wanted something lighter.

But fortunately, when Marley saw what Lisa was eating, she helped herself to a pastry as well and ignored everything else. She brought her coffee and plate to where Lisa was sitting and they chatted as they ate. Marley told her about her day in town and how she'd stopped into Izzy's shop.

"We agreed to meet for coffee next week. I'm excited to help her. If it goes well, I was thinking maybe I could use her shop as a case study of sorts and possibly do some consulting work, with other companies that are looking to go online or improve what they are already doing."

"That sounds like it could be an ideal fit for you. And you can do consulting work from anywhere since the business is online, right?" Lisa asked.

Marley nodded. "Yes. Though I do like to meet people in person when possible and actually see their business and get a feel for it. Walking into Izzy's store gave me immediate insight into who she is, what her brand is, and how that could translate online. This will be a fun project for me."

"It sounds perfect and will keep you busy while you're here."

"Yes, and not too busy. I'll still have plenty of time to explore the island and to relax."

"Speaking of relaxing, Rhett and I want you to join us for dinner tonight. I made a huge lasagna last night and some fresh garlic bread."

Marley looked tempted. "Are you sure? I don't want to intrude."

Lisa laughed. "Don't be silly. It will be fun. I made tons and we have plenty of wine. I even picked up tiramisu from the Italian bakery yesterday. That's Rhett's favorite. We're being a little bad for breakfast. I'm just going to have salad for lunch, so I can splurge at dinner. So, you'll join us?"

"I'd love to. I'll eat light at lunch ,too, just a bit of soup or something. This was so good, I almost feel like taking a nap. I'm going to head up to my room and curl up with a book, I think. And I might try to tackle knitting this afternoon. I bought a book, needles, yarn, everything I need, and I signed up for a class too, next Tuesday morning."

"Hmm. Maybe I'll join you on Tuesday, if there's room. I'll call on Monday. It's been ages since I've tried to knit. I could use few classes as a refresher."

"I hope you will. That will be fun." Marley stood. "What time should I come down for dinner?"

Lisa thought for a moment. "Let's say six. We'll have some wine and cheese first."

Marley headed upstairs, while Lisa poured herself another cup of coffee. She knew Rhett would be in any moment. He was out shoveling. She'd offered to help, but he'd insisted that he could handle it. He was just doing the walkway as they had a plow service that had already come and plowed and shoveled out their cars. They paid a little extra for that, but it was well worth it.

Lisa had just settled back in her chair with her fresh cup of coffee and was checking Facebook on her phone when the front door opened and Rhett came in. He took off his coat and shoes before joining her. His hair was mussed from the wind and his cheeks were bright red from the cold. She thought he looked adorable. He handed her a stack of letters. She'd forgotten to bring in the mail from the day before.

"How is it out there?" she asked as Rhett poured himself a black coffee before joining her. He wasn't a big breakfast eater. He usually had coffee first, then maybe a bagel or a piece of toast.

"It's not too bad right now. Looks like the calm before the storm though, so I'm glad I got that done now before the second wave comes later today."

"I think the worst of it is behind us, though. They are only saying another inch or two tonight. It might get very cold though." Lisa glanced at the mail, which was mostly bills and clothing catalogs. Something from the town of Nantucket caught her eye, and she slid open the envelope, which was addressed to her and the Beach Plum Cove Inn. She pulled out a single sheet of paper, a letter, read it once and then again out loud.

"Rhett, listen to this."

Dear Mrs. Hodges, it has come to our attention that you are in violation of the town of Nantucket's Board of Health, which prohibits a bed-and-breakfast from serving hot food. We have reports that on more than one occasion, you have served hot items such as quiche or waffles. This is a warning that you must cease and desist the serving of hot food immediately and you are fined accordingly.

Rhett frowned. "You can't serve quiche? Are they serious? Is this something new?"

"I have no idea. I just assumed it was fine to serve quiche and waffles. Who would ever think you couldn't do that?"

"What else does it say?" Rhett asked.

"Not much. Hold on. Okay, it says hot food can only be served if it is prepared in a commercial kitchen that is on the premises."

"Hmm, well there goes that idea then."

"What idea?"

"I was thinking you could bake your quiches at my restaurant, then bring them here. But they want the commercial kitchen on the premises. How could this have been missed? Didn't they come here and inspect before granting you a license?"

"They did, but now that I think of it, the usual person was out sick, so they had someone filling in that kept getting phone calls, so she was a little distracted. And they came later in the morning. It had been a busy day, and the quiche was gone, so it looked like I was compliant. Just fruit, muffins, coffee and juice were left."

"Well, that's too bad. People love your quiche. And you mention it in your ads, too?"

"Actually, we don't. Kate suggested that I not be too specific in case I didn't feel like making quiche or eggs one day. So, we just said something like a lovely continental breakfast."

"I wonder how they found out then?" Rhett said.

Lisa thought about it and had an idea.

"People often mention the quiche in reviews on TripAdvisor and other places. And I'm sure my competitors, Violet and others, check out their own reviews as well as others and saw it. So someone—I don't know who—but someone notified them."

"Well, it's just a fine. Could be worse. At least they didn't shut you down. And think, now it's less work for you." Rhett tried to get her to look on the bright side.

"I suppose. Oh well. On another note, Marley is going to join us for dinner tonight. I thought that might be fun for her. Us too. I told her around six."

LISA OPENED THE DOOR WHEN MARLEY KNOCKED AT SIX o'clock sharp. Marley handed her a bottle of wine as she stepped inside.

"Oh, thank you. You didn't have to bring anything. I didn't expect it."

"I stopped at that Bradford's Liquors when I was out

yesterday and picked up a few bottles of wine. Decoy is one of my favorites. It's a really smooth cabernet, made by the same people that make Duckhorn, which is fabulous, but expensive. My ex used to always order it when we went out. Decoy is more my speed."

"I can't wait to try it. Let's have it now. Come into the kitchen. I just put out the cheese and crackers."

Lisa led the way to where Rhett was already sitting at the kitchen island, eyeing the cheese.

"Look at the wine Marley brought for us. Have you had this one?"

"I have. We actually have that in the restaurant and Duckhorn too. We sell a lot more of the Decoy."

Lisa opened the wine and poured them all a glass, and they joined Rhett at the island. "We'll eat in about a half hour or so. I just put the lasagna in the oven to heat up."

They chatted easily as they sipped wine and snacked on the cheese and crackers. Lisa remembered that she needed to update Marley about the breakfast situation.

"So, I found out this morning that evidently I'm not supposed to be serving any hot food—which includes quiche, waffles, the puff pastry dish I served this morning. I might add some cold cereals to try to make up for it. I am sorry about that."

"Don't be sorry. It's not your fault. As delicious as the egg thing this morning was, I am much better off eating lighter, so it's totally fine by me. As soon as this snow is gone, I want to get out and walk along the beach. I could easily see myself gaining weight this month."

Lisa was relieved but still disappointed. She enjoyed making her quiches and other hot foods for her guests.

"You know, I've been thinking about this a bit," Rhett said. "If you're interested, we could probably renovate your kitchen pretty easily to comply with what qualifies as a commercial kitchen. We could upgrade your existing kitchen or another option is we could do an addition, so it's connected to but separate from the kitchen. That way, if you ever wanted to hire some help, you could have a separate entrance."

"Hmm. That seems like a big undertaking just to be able to make one quiche every few days," Lisa said.

"Well, I was thinking you might want to go a bit bigger than that. Which is another advantage of the separate kitchen. You love to cook and especially in the winter, you have free time on your hands. What if you made some quiches and other items and sold them?"

"Sold them? To who?" Lisa was curious, but a bit confused about what he had mind. But Marley chimed in.

"That's a great idea. If it's something you think you'd like to do. You could sell to local restaurants."

"Like my place, for instance," Rhett said with a grin. "We could sell your key lime pie easily. I've thought about putting that on the menu and haven't gotten around to it. It's one more thing they don't have time to make. But if it's done for us…"

"There's also online sales, too. Gourmet food is a huge seller. You could do it direct or through a food site like Gold Belly."

"What's Gold Belly?" Lisa had no idea what she was referring to.

"Oh, you are in for a treat. Look it up, but don't do it when you're hungry or you'll get in trouble. Restaurants and food shops all over the country sell their most famous dishes through Gold Belly. You can get lobster rolls from Legal Seafoods, a cannoli kit from Mike's Pastry in the North End, Banana Cream Pie from Magnolia Bakery down South."

"Really? That does sound like something I'd like. I'll check it out."

Lisa started feeling a little excited about the idea. The bed-and-breakfast was great, but it didn't take up much of her time. Maybe there was something more she could do.

"How difficult would it be to get something like this going?" she asked both Rhett and Marley.

"Well, you'd have to get on someone's schedule for the construction. Though you do have an in there." Rhett grinned. Lisa's son, Chase, owned and operated a construction company on Nantucket. He'd done the initial renovation to convert her home into a bed-and-breakfast. He could probably do a small addition pretty easily.

"I could check with Chase. This is his slow time of year."

"And I can help you make sure it's compliant, like I've done with all my restaurants. I can get us a discount on the equipment too."

"I could help you put a plan together for online sales, if you think you might want to do that," Marley offered.

"Thank you. I'm going to sleep on this. But it feels like it might be a good thing. And I'm lucky to have both of you with your expertise to help. It kind of feels like a sign."

Marley smiled. "It does, doesn't it?"

CHAPTER 10

The thrill of the nor'easter wore off by Saturday morning when Izzy woke up to a dark, cold house. They'd had fun the night before. She and Mia had stayed up late watching old movies, snacking on junk food and drinking hot chocolate. They loved watching the snow falling over the harbor and kept the outside light on so they could see it coming down. It was blowing furiously and they could see the trees swaying and whipping in the heavy wind.

The power had stayed on, so they thought they'd been lucky, but sometime while they were sleeping it went out. Izzy guessed it was soon after they went to bed because the heat had obviously been off for a while. She checked the thermostat, and it was only sixty degrees. Ten degrees cooler than normal. She got up and dressed in layers and realized she had no way to make hot coffee. But then, with relief, she remembered that Mia's stove was gas, so she could at least heat some water for a cup of tea.

She was curled up on the sofa, wrapped in one of Mia's fleece throws, cupping the mug in her hands to feel its warmth and occasionally taking a sip when Mia padded into the room, followed by Penny. Mia looked half-awake as she looked around for her hat and gloves, found her coat and boots and went to take Penny outside.

"I can make you a cup of hot tea, if you want?" Izzy offered.

"If you do, I will love you forever," Mia said.

Izzy heated up some water on the stove and when Mia and Penny returned, she poured it into a mug and added the tea bag. Mia joined her in the living room and they looked at each other miserably as they sipped their tea.

"This isn't fun anymore," Izzy said as she looked around the dark room.

"No, it's not. Maybe the power will come on soon though."

"I hope so. But if not, it's only going to get colder by tonight. We need a Plan B."

"Sam and his family picked a great week to go to Florida," Mia said. Her boyfriend Sam, his two girls and his parents left a few days ago, missing the storm completely.

"I ran into Will yesterday on my way home. He said we're welcome to stay with him if we lose power. He has a generator and a wood stove."

"That's tempting. His place has plenty of room for all of us too. Let's give it a few hours and see if the power comes on."

Izzy's phone rang a few minutes later, and she saw that it was Rick.

"Hi there. Do you have power where you are?"

"No. Mine went out last night. I hear it won't be back on for most of us until tomorrow. I think they're waiting until this new storm is done too. Why don't you come here? I can come get you."

"I'm not going to leave Mia, and if you don't have power either, doesn't make sense for us to leave."

"I suppose you're right. If you change your mind, let me know."

"I will. Thanks, Rick."

Mia laughed. "He doesn't have power either, but wanted you to go to his place?"

"Yeah. If we're going to leave, it will be to go somewhere warm."

A FEW HOURS LATER, THE TEMPERATURE HAD DROPPED TO fifty-eight and Izzy was about to call Will when her phone rang and he was calling her to check in.

"I was just about to call you!"

"Do you guys want to come here? I have a roaring fire, the generator is fired up, and I was thinking about making burgers for dinner. Sound good? I can come anytime to get you both."

"That all sounds wonderful. I think we're ready now." Izzy glanced at Mia, who had Penny in her lap for warmth and was still shivering. She nodded and said, "Ask if it's okay if Penny comes too?"

Will heard her and laughed. "Of course it is. I'll leave in a few minutes."

WILL'S TRUCK PULLED UP TWENTY MINUTES LATER, AND they all climbed in. Izzy got in the front and Mia in the back, with Penny on her lap. The truck was nice and warm, and Izzy realized how cold they'd been. There was almost no one on the road as they drove the short distance to Will's house.

It didn't take long to get to his house, and Izzy smiled as they pulled into the driveway and saw the lights on and the smoke rising from the chimney. Will's house looked wonderful. They went inside and Will showed them where his guest bedrooms were and he gave them the grand tour. They'd been there a few times over the summer for cookouts, but had mostly been outside or just in the kitchen.

Will worked in construction and in addition to specializing in restoration work, he also built custom furniture. Over the past few years, he'd been working on his house in between projects. He'd picked the house up at a bargain price, as there had been a fire and the owners didn't want to deal with rebuilding. So, it was the perfect property for Will. It was bigger than he needed, with four bedrooms, but it was a deal he couldn't pass up.

All the rooms had gleaming hard wood floors, but the

room Will was the most proud of was his office. It had wall-to-wall built-in book cases, cabinets and a desk, and he'd made all of it. The wood was dark and polished and Izzy was so impressed.

"I can't believe you did this yourself. It's really beautiful work, Will."

Mia chimed in too. "It's stunning."

He looked a bit embarrassed but also pleased by the compliments.

"Thank you, both. So, that's the grand tour. Are you guys hungry? I could make my famous juicy Lucy burgers."

Izzy's stomach immediately growled, and she laughed. "Yes, please. What can we do to help?"

"Maybe you two can throw a salad together while I put the burgers on the grill. See what you can find in the fridge. And help yourself to anything you want to drink. There's wine, beer, and bottled water."

Mia poured herself a glass of red wine while Izzy found a water and they searched to see what Will had for salad. Quite a bit, as it turned out. They made a salad with lettuce, cucumber, tomatoes, onion, and avocado and tossed it with Italian dressing. Will's burgers, with the cheese stuffed in the middle, were as good as ever and they had a good time laughing and chatting as they ate at the big round table in his kitchen, while Penny slept by Mia's feet. She'd fed Penny before Will arrived, so she wasn't begging for their food.

Izzy and Mia insisted on doing the dishes while Will went to clean up his grill. He came back in the kitchen with a deck of cards and suggested they play a few rounds of pitch, which they all loved. A few rounds turned into a few more as they decided to up the stakes and toss in a dollar each, winner take all. It was a fun game and a competitive one, but none of them took it too seriously. Mia was the lucky one with a winning streak that had her winning three games in a row.

"I'm so glad you guys decided to come here. I would have been bored by myself," Will admitted.

"And we would have been miserable and freezing. So, thank you. This has been fun. We should play cards more often."

"We should. Speaking of games, are we all on for trivia on Tuesday? The snow should be long gone by then," Will said. At least a few times a month Izzy, Mia, Sam and Will met downtown for dinner and a night of team trivia.

"I'm up for it. And I think Sam will be too. They fly back on Monday," Mia said.

"I'm in," Izzy said.

"So, you like Izzy's idea to expand the store? She said you're going to help open up the wall between the unit next door?" Mia said.

Izzy knew that Mia still had some reservations but thought highly of Will's opinion.

"Like it? I think I may have actually suggested it. I think it's a fantastic idea."

Izzy laughed. "He did. He stopped in the day I found out that the woman next to me wasn't going to renew her lease. It had crossed my mind of course and I was wondering if it might make sense and he just came right out and said, 'You should grab that.'"

"I did. It seemed obvious to me. There's so much foot traffic right there and every woman I know on Nantucket raves about Izzy's store."

"They do?" Izzy hadn't heard that before.

He nodded. "Yes. Everyone. Caroline used to say your store was the only reasonably priced one downtown that had nice stuff. And I was at Chase's office just the other day as we're working on a project together and his wife Beth walked in with one of your bags. She'd gone there on her lunch break and she said you have the best shoes. She showed us the black boots she bought."

Izzy smiled. "Those boots have been popular. That is so nice to hear."

"He's right, Izzy. You do an amazing job with that store," Mia said. "You know I'm more cautious, but I do think it's a good idea. I'm excited for you."

Izzy felt happy tears well up and laughed. "Thank you. Sorry I'm a little emotional…It really is true about the hormones. I'm happy, though. It's all good."

"Now, we just have to get you to end things with Rick once and for all," Mia said and then immediately looked as though she regretted her words when a strange look came across Will's face. Izzy knew her sister had spoken impulsively.

"You're not back with him, are you?" He sounded shocked and disappointed.

"No. I just met him for dinner the other night. I'd agreed to see him, to talk. He seems to be doing well. He went through an anger management course, for twelve weeks and he really does seem better."

"So, you want to try to work things out? I get it. You two have a baby coming. You could be a family. If that's what you want."

"I don't think that's what I want. It is hard for me to believe that someone could change that much. There was a time that we were happy though, and as you said, we do have a baby coming." Izzy sighed. "I told him that we could go out again and take things really slow. Mia is actually going to come with us next weekend, which will be a good test, to see how that goes."

"Hmm. Well, I just want to see you happy, Izzy. And safe." Will yawned and Izzy felt the pull to do the same. She glanced at the time and was surprised to see how late it was, almost midnight.

"I should take Penny out before we head to bed," Mia said.

Will stood. "I'm going to call it a night. I'll see you both in the morning. If you get up before me, coffee is in the cabinet by the stove."

"Thanks again, Will." Izzy watched them both leave the room and slowly got up and made her way to bed, too. They'd had such a fun night until Mia mentioning Rick had really put a damper on the mood.

———

WHILE THEY WERE SITTING AROUND THE KITCHEN TABLE the next morning, sipping coffee and eating buttered toast, the generator clicked off as the power came back on. Will fired up his laptop, checked the outage map online and saw that most of Nantucket, including the downtown marina area where Izzy and Mia lived, was back up too.

Once they finished eating, Will drove them home. They thanked him again and planned to see him at trivia on Tuesday. It was still cold when they first walked in the condo. The temperature had fallen a few more degrees, but it didn't take long to warm up, and as she always did whenever the power went out, Izzy really appreciated it when it came back on.

A text message came through from Rick. "Is your power back?

"Yes, just came on a little bit ago. You?"

"Same. Went to my buddy Mark's last night."

"We went to one of Mia's friends that had a generator. Glad to be home."

"Cool. Will be in touch end of the week."

Izzy breathed a sigh of relief. She was glad he hadn't asked which friend. Izzy didn't want to lie, but she knew he wouldn't have understood if she'd said Will. Before they broke up, Rick had accused her of having something going on with Will. And when she'd denied it, he'd still insisted that Will was interested. She'd told him then that he was being ridiculous, and that Will was just a good friend. Someone that had always been there for her. And when things got ugly with Rick, it was Will who got her away from him and brought her to Mia's.

Izzy knew that Mia was hoping that something might

happen between her and Will, but Izzy just couldn't think of him that way. She wasn't ready to date anyone, and she was confused by her feelings for Rick. Intellectually, she knew it was probably best to firmly end things. But they had so much history, and it was hard to just turn that off. She couldn't walk away completely yet. Part of her would always wonder if maybe things could have worked out. If Rick really was able to change and be a better man. She owed it to both of them and to their baby to find out if it was possible.

CHAPTER 11

After the nor'easter on Friday, followed by more snow on Saturday and then again another inch on Sunday, by Monday, Kate was entirely sick of it and feeling grumpy and stir-crazy. She didn't mind working from home, until she did. And every few weeks she was sick of her own company and needed to be around other people. That's when she'd take her laptop and go work downtown at one of the coffee shops for a few hours. The white noise of people talking around her and coming and going gave her some much-needed energy.

So, on Monday, soon after Jack left for work, Kate decided she needed a coffee shop day. She went to the Corner Table and got herself a caramel-topped macchiato and a raspberry scone. She settled at a table in the middle of the room, plugged in her laptop to an outlet on the floor, and opened her manuscript. The coffee shop was busy and the hum of people all around her made her happy. The noise didn't bother her at all. She was able to block it out and lose herself in her story.

She was so deep into it that she didn't hear someone calling her name at first.

"Kate! I don't want to disturb you, as you look like you are intent on your writing, but I just wanted to say hi."

Kate looked up and smiled when she saw who it was —Angela, one of her favorite people. She hadn't known her long, but they'd become close friends right away and Angela was married to another one of her favorite people, Philippe, who was the kind of famous mystery writer that Kate could only dream of being one day. The two of them were very much opposites, but it worked and Kate was happy for them both.

"Have a seat. I can take a break for a bit. I just had to get out of the house. How are you?"

Angela sat across from her and stirred a packet of sugar into her coffee.

"I'm good! I have a little time before I have to be to my next client. This week is quiet with people either cancelling or being out of town."

"It seems like forever since I've seen you. How is Philippe?"

"He's good. He's actually been in LA for the past two weeks. He comes home tomorrow."

"So, he totally missed all the snow. Were you nervous being there by yourself?" They lived in a huge home on the water. Beautiful, but Kate wasn't sure she'd have wanted to be there by herself in a snowstorm.

"No, not really. The house is alarmed and has a generator. Ken was over on Friday and cooked up a storm, so I had delicious meals all weekend that I just had to heat up." Ken was Philippe's personal chef that catered all of their parties and dropped food off every other week.

"I love to cook, but I think I could get used to someone cooking for me too," Kate said.

"Ken has spoiled us. Philippe isn't a cook. I like to cook sometimes, but when he's away, I usually end up working late and am too tired to do more than heat up a can of soup."

"Well, when I get rich and famous, maybe I'll borrow Ken," Kate teased.

Angela smiled. "How are you feeling? You look great."

"Thanks. Oh, I have some big news. Jack and I just found out on Friday that we're having twins. A boy and a girl."

"Wow, that's awesome. How exciting!"

"Thank you. It was a bit of a shock." Kate told her about the scare she'd had.

"So, I guess it's a fairly common thing. I'm supposed to rest as much as possible. So, I probably won't stay here too long. I just had to get out of the house."

"I bet. I can understand that."

"Enough about me. What's new and exciting with you?"

"Not much. I'm looking forward to Philippe coming home. I don't like it when he's gone this long. He doesn't have any travel planned for at least six months or so though, so that's good. Work has been busy. I hired another girl last week." Angela ran a cleaning business that was growing fast.

"That's great. We really need a girls' night. Maybe I'll have an appetizer party soon. It's been a while since we all got together. What do you think?"

"I'd love it. Just let me know when and what I can bring and I'll be there."

Kristen stopped by for breakfast Tuesday morning and Lisa introduced her to Marley, who was heading back up to her room. Lisa had called the knitting shop the day before to see if there was room in the next day's class. There was, so Lisa and Marley were going to head into town a little before ten.

"I'm sorry I don't have anything hot to offer you, honey." Lisa told her about the Board of Health letter and the fine. Of all her children, Kristen was the pickiest eater and rarely ate much for breakfast, so she didn't think she'd mind. But still, it annoyed her that she couldn't offer hot food.

Kristen smiled. "Mom, please don't worry about it. A piece of toast is all I usually have, so this is more than fine. I am sorry though. I know how much you like to cook for everyone."

"Well, Rhett had some ideas that we're going to look

into. I'll keep you posted on what we decide. How did you and Tyler survive the storm?"

"We actually had a good time. I stayed at his place and we just hunkered down and watched movies. He had his new wood stove going, and it was toasty warm. And we never lost power. I know we were lucky there."

"I'm glad. Tyler's good? His writing is going well?" Tyler was an alcoholic and when Kristen first started dating him, Lisa had been concerned, even though he was sober at the time. She worried about what would happen if he fell off the wagon. She knew that would be hard for both of them. And when his mother died unexpectedly, Tyler relapsed and hid it for a long time before getting help. But Lisa gave him credit. He went to a treatment center, got the help he needed, and with Kristen's support, they were both doing well. They weren't engaged yet, but Lisa had a feeling it was coming at some point.

"He's doing great, and he just finished his latest project last week and sent it off to his editor, so now he's relaxing and making notes for his next book."

Lisa was glad to hear it. "Oh, I know what I wanted to talk to you about. We need to plan a baby shower for your sister. Any ideas on where and when?"

"Funny you should mention that. I just talked to her on my way over here, and she invited me over for one of her appetizer parties next week. It's Thursday night. What if we turned it into a baby shower? She'd never suspect it—and it would be fun to surprise her."

Lisa thought about that for a moment. She liked the

idea. "Are you sure she won't mind having her party crashed by her mother and her friends?"

Kristen laughed. "Hardly. She loves you guys. I think she'd love it once she got past the initial shock. If you want to invite Sue and Paige, I'll tell everyone else. Do you have any idea what she wants?"

"She needs everything. I'll make a list and send it to you and you can email it to everyone so we can make sure she doesn't get too many duplicates—especially on the bigger things. Although there are two babies, so I guess duplicates are fine!"

"Perfect. This is going to be fun." Kristen stayed for another cup of coffee and then headed home to her studio to start work on a new painting. Lisa put everything away and was ready to go when Marley knocked on the door.

THEY ARRIVED AT ELOISE'S KNITTING SHOP AT FIVE OF ten. Eloise greeted them and directed them into the adjoining room where the classes were held.

"Help yourself to coffee or tea in the corner and then grab a seat. We'll get started in a few minutes."

There was a big round table in the middle of the room with ten seats around it. Half of the table was full, so they set their purses on two seats, then went to get coffee. Lisa had just taken a sip when she saw a familiar face walk into the room and almost choked on her coffee.

Especially when the woman and her friend sat next to Lisa.

"Lisa, so good to see you. It's been a while," the woman said a little too sweetly. Lisa was sure of it now that she was the one that had notified the Board of Health. She couldn't imagine who else would have done it.

Lisa noticed Marley's curious gaze and hurriedly introduced her.

"Marley, this is Violet. She owns a bed-and-breakfast in Beach Plum Cove too." Understanding flashed across her face. Marley smiled and held out her hand. "It's so nice to meet you."

"This is my sister, Barbara." Violet introduced the other woman that was with her.

"Marley is staying with us this month," Lisa said.

"A whole month! This time of year." Violet waited for more of an explanation, but neither Lisa nor Marley provided one. She looked like she was going to say more, but then Eloise started the class and for the next forty-five minutes, they didn't have time to chat. Lisa and Marley needed to pay close attention, and Violet seemed even more lost than they were. Eloise was wonderful though and walked around the table, helping each person as they needed it. Before they knew it, the class was over. As they gathered up their yarn and needles, Violet turned to Lisa.

"I heard about what happened. It really is a silly rule that we can't serve hot food, isn't it?"

Lisa met her gaze. "It is. How did you hear about it?"

Violet smiled. "Well, it was in the paper, of course. All health violations are printed in the weekly paper."

Lisa sighed. Violet was right. Great, now the whole town knew she'd been fined. "Right. I forgot about that. It's ok. Maybe this will turn out to be a good thing."

Violet looked confused. "How could it possibly be a good thing?"

Lisa smiled, the same overly sweet smile that Violet had first sent her way. "Well, everything happens for a reason, they say. We'll just have to see what develops."

Lisa and Marley swept out of the room and as soon as they were on the street, Marley burst into laughter.

"The look on her face was priceless. She is dying to know what you are up to."

"I know. That was fun. I don't want to say anything until it's done and fully licensed. If she knew what I was up to, I wouldn't put it past her to try to make things even more difficult."

CHAPTER 12

Will was the first to arrive at the Rose and Crown Pub Tuesday night. He'd texted Izzy earlier to confirm the time, and they agreed on six. He was usually a few minutes early, and Izzy and her sister were almost always a few minutes late. He liked to tease them about it sometimes. He wasn't going to tease them today though. He was still feeling a little bad about being short with Izzy when Mia brought Rick up the other night. It had just caught him totally by surprise. Izzy hadn't mentioned Rick in ages, and he was sure that she was done with him.

Will had been biding his time, waiting for the right moment to let Izzy know how he felt about her. He hadn't known himself until recently. He'd always thought of Izzy as a good friend, a beautiful, kind friend, but one that had a serious boyfriend, so she was off-limits for those kinds of thoughts. Until she wasn't. But he knew from spending time with her that she wasn't ready to date yet. He'd thought that she was just focused on the baby as that was a huge change, but he hadn't realized that she hadn't moved on from Rick yet and worse that she was considering giving him another chance. The thought of it made his blood boil, and he wasn't the one with anger management issues.

He just thought that she deserved better than Rick Savage. Even if she didn't want to date Will, she still deserved better than Rick. Will wondered if maybe Izzy's hormones were making her a little crazy and confused. That was the only explanation that made any sense to him.

But, as he saw her walking toward him, he put the dark thoughts out of his mind and promised himself not to mention Rick or anything negative. He just wanted to have a fun night and enjoy the company of his friends, especially Izzy. She took his breath away as she caught his eye and smiled. Izzy's smile was huge. It filled her whole face and lit up her eyes and made him feel happy. He smiled back as Izzy, Mia and Sam made their way toward him.

"Hi Will. Have you been here long?" Izzy asked.

"No. I just got here and let the hostess know we need a table. She's getting one ready for us now."

The hostess returned a moment later and led them to a booth in the bar area where the trivia was held. There was already a good-sized crowd gathered. Trivia nights were popular on Nantucket. It was something fun to do in the middle of the week.

Izzy sat next to him and as she took off her coat, he

caught a whiff of her shampoo. Green apple. It smelled fresh and clean. She looked gorgeous, too, in a pretty, pale blue sweater. Her blonde hair was so long, longer than he'd ever seen it before. And no-one had curls like Izzy. They fell in long spirals down to the middle of her back. To him, she was the prettiest girl in the world and definitely the one he was most attracted to. He just liked being around her and every week, he looked forward to Tuesday nights.

"What's everyone in the mood for? Any interest in sharing a pizza? It's buy-one-get-one-free tonight," Izzy said.

"I'll do pizza," Will said. He didn't care what he ate, really. If Izzy wanted pizza, that worked for him.

"I think I want a burger," Sam said.

"I'm thinking salad, maybe," Mia said.

They put their order in when the waitress came. Will and Sam ordered draft beers, Mia got a glass of wine and Izzy surprised him by ordering a Shirley Temple.

She laughed at the look on his face. "I know I'm too old for it, but I've always liked them and since I can't have a real drink…"

He smiled. "I just had a project rescheduled, so if you like, I can work on your shop construction this weekend."

Izzy looked pleased. "Really? That would be great. I can close the store at two if you want to come any time after that, and I'm closed on Sundays this time of year, anyway."

"I'll plan to come by around two then."

The trivia host dropped off their scoring sheets and

answer pads. As usual, their team name was Nantucket Threads, after Izzy's store.

Over dinner, Sam told them about his trip to Florida. He'd gone with his parents and two young daughters to Disney World and Universal Studios.

"What did the girls like most?" Izzy asked.

Sam laughed. "That's easy. The Harry Potter ride at Universal. I think that was my favorite too. It was quite a ride. They automatically take your picture half-way through and the expressions on our faces were priceless. My mother came with us and her eyes were shut, Becky looked terrified, Sarah was laughing, and I had a stupid grin on my face. My mother has already framed it and hung it on the wall."

"That sounds fun. I've never been to Universal Studios. Maybe someday I'll take peanut there."

"Peanut?" Will laughed.

"Well, I don't have a name for him or her yet."

"You're not going to find out what it is?" Sam asked.

Izzy shook her head. "No. I want to be surprised."

"I keep telling her that it will be a surprise no matter when she finds out. Why not know now so she can prepare better?" Mia said sensibly.

"That's what you would do. It would kill you not to know," Izzy said.

Mia laughed. "You're absolutely right."

"For me, it's something to look forward to." Izzy had a serene look on her face. The two sisters were so different, yet they were very close and Will liked them both, though in very different ways. He thought of Mia almost like a sister and a very good friend. He was still trying to figure out exactly how he felt about Izzy, but it definitely wasn't sisterly. For now, they were friends—in time, who knew. Before Izzy found out she was pregnant, when she'd first left Rick, Will had thought once or twice that he'd sensed a vibe from her, but the feeling was fleeting and he wasn't sure if he'd imagined it, and if it was just wishful thinking on his side.

He hadn't felt any kind of vibe since and Izzy had shifted into expectant mother mode, almost like she was hunkering down and getting ready. He didn't think dating was on her radar at all, so to hear she was going on a date with Rick was disconcerting. He hoped that they would have a horrible time, then felt like a terrible friend for feeling that way. But he couldn't help himself. The sooner that Rick Savage was out of the picture, the better. Though with a child between them, Will knew that Rick would never be totally out of Izzy's life. He just hoped that it would be a co-parenting relationship only. If they did get back together, Will knew, based on what he'd seen before, that it wouldn't be good for Izzy. But he also knew that she needed to come to that realization on her own.

Trivia started just as they were finishing their dinners. There was almost a whole pizza left over and Will insisted that Izzy take it home.

There were eighteen teams playing and while they got a few answers right, it wasn't one of their better nights. They often ended up in one of the top three spots at the end of the night, but tonight they landed in the bottom two.

"We are bad tonight," Izzy said and laughed.

"We keep second-guessing ourselves," Mia agreed. And they had. More than once, one of them said the right answer then changed it at the last minute to something else.

But it was still a fun time, all-around. Will said his goodbyes when they left soon after trivia ended. He was looking forward to Saturday, when he'd see Izzy again at her shop.

CHAPTER 13

I zzy was thrilled that Marley called and set a time to meet on Thursday before work. They agreed to meet at the Corner Table coffee shop, chat for a bit and then walk over to the store, so Marley could get a better look around.

When Thursday morning came, Izzy made sure she was on time and arrived at the coffee shop at five of nine. She got in line to order and as she reached the counter, Marley appeared and Izzy ordered coffee and pumpkin spice muffins for them both.

They found a table in a quiet area and chatted about the storm and what they'd both been up to since then, as they ate their muffins. When they finished, Marley pulled out what looked like an iPad, but Izzy realized it was something else as once it was fired up, Marley took notes on it using a special pen.

"What is that?"

"It's called the reMarkable. You write on it and then

with a click you can turn it into text and email your notes to yourself. I love it." She smiled. "So, tell me everything I need to know about Nantucket Threads. Who is your customer?"

Izzy thought about that. "It depends on the time of year and I don't think I really have one profile, one buyer persona. That's what they call it, right?"

Marley looked impressed. "Yes. I never knew that myself until we hired some MBA types as we grew the marketing division and they explained how buyer personas were constructed and what to do with them. You basically figure out who your customers are and how you can better reach them, and the persona is a typical customer. So if you learn that quite a few like to knit, for instance, then your marketing strategy could include advertising on knitting-related websites. That kind of thing."

"That's a good explanation," Izzy said. "I bought a book on marketing and the term was mentioned, but I wasn't sure what it meant. Most of the tourists that wander in are right off the boat and are just window shopping. If they buy, it's usually the Nantucket gear, the hats and sweatshirts."

Marley laughed. "Like I did."

"Right. But you also fit into my main demographic, too. You bought the fleece pants and comfy socks. Women from their thirties to sixties are my core buyers. They like reasonably priced sweaters, cute shoes, trendy tops and flattering dresses. I buy what I love and so far, it's worked out okay."

"You are your buyer too, so that helps a lot. Are you doing any online sales now?"

"Not really. Well, actually I do get calls now and then from people that have been in the store and want to buy something they saw. Usually after someone saw an item that was bought here and they want another or want to give as a gift."

"And how do you handle those sales?"

Izzy grinned. "I drop everything and mail it off to them. Probably not too smart, right?"

"Actually, that tells me that customer service is important to you. And good customer service, putting the customer first is how companies do very well. Look at Amazon with their fast delivery and easy returns."

"That's true. They make it really easy to buy from them."

"Exactly. That's the key. Make it a great, easy experience and you'll be very happy with how things go."

Izzy started to feel excited. "Do you really think I have a chance to grow my business with the website? Part of me is nervous that I won't make back my investment. I'm using most of my savings to do this," she admitted.

"There's never a guarantee in business. But you have an advantage in that you already have a successful store. If we put lots of images of the store and Nantucket on the site, that will help potential customers feel comfortable ordering."

"I didn't even think about putting shots of Nantucket on the site. But that makes sense. The waterfront area is pretty and quaint with the cobblestone streets."

"Nantucket is part of your image. It's a beautiful place, and expensive. You have beautiful things that look expensive but are affordable. That's a powerful hook. They won't just be buying a sweatshirt. They will be buying the whole Nantucket experience, which is very appealing to many people."

"I wouldn't have thought of any of this. I'm so glad you stopped in my store."

Marley smiled. "I'm glad, too. I have a lot of free time on my hands this month, and I'd been wondering about what I wanted to do next. So, I'd say it's fortunate for both of us. Are you ready to go walk around the store? I'm curious to hear your plans for the expansion."

They had about thirty minutes before Nantucket Threads officially opened at ten, and in that time, Izzy showed Marley all around and explained what she had in mind for the space next door. Marley asked a lot of questions and Izzy's head was spinning at all the different options available for selling online—Shopify, Woocommerce, Payhip and so many more.

"I didn't realize there were so many options," Izzy said.

"I know I'm throwing a lot at you, but I just wanted to give you an overview. Some of these will be better for you than others, and I'll send you an email outlining my recommendations and suggestions on how to get started."

Marley left just before ten and said she'd be in touch soon. Izzy put the open sign in the window and settled in behind the counter. She was feeling very lucky that Marley had decided to walk in her store and was willing to help her. Because after spending time with her, Izzy realized she had a lot to learn—more than she realized. She was looking forward to seeing Marley's recommendations and to seeing Will on Saturday. It would all seem more real once he opened up the wall to the shop next door. Izzy turned on her laptop. She needed to get busy placing some orders to fill up all that space.

CHAPTER 14

L isa made a hearty ham, onion, pepper and cheddar cheese quiche for breakfast Thursday morning. When she brought it into the dining room, Rhett was already sitting there sipping his usual black coffee and raised his eyebrow.

"Living dangerously, I see? What if the Board of Health stops by?" he teased her.

Lisa laughed. "Let them. I made this for us. We have company coming. Beth and Chase are stopping by to discuss the kitchen expansion, and I told them to come early and with a big appetite."

Marley walked into the room and said hello before heading to pour a cup of coffee.

"My son and his wife are coming, so I made us something hot. Please help yourself," Lisa said.

"I was just going to have some fruit and try to be good, but if you insist."

Chase and Beth arrived a few minutes later and when they were seated, Lisa introduced Marley to everyone.

"Chase is going to help me build a commercial kitchen. I might try making quiches and pies and possibly other things to sell at some local restaurants and shops," Lisa told her.

Marley looked pleased. "You decided to do it, good. I wasn't sure if you were serious about it."

Lisa laughed. "I wasn't sure either, but the more I thought about it, the more I liked the idea. And Rhett says he'll buy my pies, so at least I'll have one customer."

"I think it's a great idea, Mom. We both do," Chase said.

"We do," Beth agreed. "I think it sounds like a fun project. Maybe whoever told on you actually did you a favor."

"I hope so."

When they finished eating, Chase took measurements in the kitchen and talked to both Rhett and Lisa. Lisa had an idea of what she wanted it to look like while Rhett knew what she needed to do to be compliant with the Board of Health. Chase took a bunch of notes, did some quick calculations and gave Lisa a rough idea of what it would cost. She knew it wasn't going to be inexpensive, but she was prepared for a higher number than what Chase gave her.

"That doesn't sound like enough, honey. You need to make money on this too."

"I have enough profit baked in. Between Rhett's contacts and mine, we can get some good discounts on both the materials and the equipment. It shouldn't take more than two weeks to get it done. But, I can't start it for a few weeks.

"He's booked solid, and there's no one I can move. Everyone's project is urgent," Beth said.

"I'm not in a huge hurry. Don't pass up a better job for mine. You can fit me in whenever, honey."

"We'll get you in soon. Beth will give you a call with a definite start date once we get closer to done on a few of these other projects."

"Great." Lisa turned to Beth. "Are you able to come next Thursday night? For Kristen's shower? I don't think I saw an email from you."

"Yes! I'm sorry, I meant to reply yesterday and got pulled away. I'm planning on it."

"Good, it will be fun. I think she'll be totally surprised."

"I think so too. I can't wait to see her face when she realizes her appetizer party is actually a shower," Beth said.

"We could make it a Jack and Jill shower, then Chase, and Rhett, and Jack, all the guys could come," Lisa said and then laughed when she saw Rhett and Chase exchange glances and Chase shook his head. "That's okay, Mom. I'm sure Kate doesn't want all of us there."

"You mean you both would prefer not to go?" Lisa asked. Chase and Rhett stayed silent. "It was just a suggestion! We'll keep it girls only—that way it's closer to what Kate was planning, anyway. So, on a different note, how is your new project going? I saw the listing online a few days ago. It looks lovely." Chase and Beth had a side business where the two of them invested in fixer-uppers when they could get a good price and then renovated and sold for a nice profit.

Beth's face lit up. "The market is crazy right now. We have an open house scheduled for Saturday and aren't showing it until then. It really does create interest. We are almost full for the day with booked appointments."

"It's priced well," Chase added. "Right at the market, so hopefully we'll get multiple offers, like on the last one." They'd had a bidding war on their last flip because it was such a good deal and there were so few properties available on Nantucket that weren't ridiculously expensive.

"Fingers crossed that you do. Do you have anything lined up after this one?" Lisa asked.

"No. Not yet, but something will turn up. It always does. This last one was an estate sale. They just wanted to get rid of it quickly, which worked for us."

Chase looked at his watch. "We should probably run. I have a call in twenty minutes with a new client."

"Thanks so much for coming by this morning," Lisa said as she walked them to the door.

"Do you know what you're going to bring for an appetizer to Kate's?" Beth asked.

"I think I'm going to make one of Kate's favorites, spiced beef cigars—it's ground beef and spices wrapped in flaky phyllo dough with a creamy dipping sauce. She said she's been craving red meat lately."

"Oh, I don't think I've had those. They sound

wonderful. I was thinking a fresh veggie tray and hummus, which totally sounds not exciting now."

"Don't be silly. Sounds perfect to me. There will be loads of rich food, I'm sure, so a lighter option is good. I love veggies and hummus."

"Okay, thanks. I'll stick to my plan, then. See you next Thursday."

Lisa returned to the kitchen where Rhett was sitting at the island, checking messages on his phone. He looked up when Lisa walked over.

"Are you feeling good about this? You're sure it's what you want to do? It's a big decision."

"I am feeling good about it. Starting the inn was a good first step for me. No one would hire me after being out of the workforce for so long. But, I feel more confident now, and with only five guest rooms, it doesn't take up much of my time. This could be a fun new challenge. Something to focus my extra time and energy on." Lisa paused before asking, "Do you think it's a good idea? You'd tell me if you think I'm crazy to even think about it?"

Rhett laughed. "I think it's a great idea, and I have no doubt you'll do well. I just wanted to make sure you were all in. It's a big investment if you're not sure."

Lisa smiled. "With a commercial kitchen, just think of the options. It will be even easier to have people over, bigger parties. I love the thought of multiple ovens."

"Good. I love the idea of being your quality tester."

Lisa leaned over and kissed him. "Of course, you do!"

CHAPTER 15

Will arrived at Izzy's shop at two o'clock sharp on Saturday. There were two customers at the register and Izzy gave him a wave as she finished ringing them up. He made his way to the rear of the store and set his heavy tool bag down. He had everything he needed to knock down part of the wall between the two shops and to make a smooth entrance way, making it one bigger store.

He walked around, looking at the clothing stacked on the shelves, while Izzy thanked her customers. As soon as they left, she flipped the open sign to closed and locked the front door, so no one else would wander in. She looked adorable, as usual. Today she was wearing jeans, a long red sweater and black boots. If he didn't know better, he never would have guessed she was pregnant. Will didn't know much about women's styles, but he knew Izzy looked sharp. She always did, though.

"Hi, Will, thanks for coming. Sorry to keep you waiting," Izzy apologized.

"Don't be silly. I'm glad you had customers. Was it busy today?"

Izzy made a face and laughed. "No. They were the first customers I've had in over an hour. Figures they'd come in right as I was getting ready to close. They were quick, though. Tourists that wanted Nantucket sweatshirts."

"No kidding? Even this time of year, huh?" Will knew it was rare for tourists in January.

"There's a few. It's still a beautiful place to get away to, at any time of year. I love the peace and quiet in winter, though it's not so good for business."

Will smiled. "I do too. Maybe once you get your website going, that will make up for the slow winter months?"

"I hope so. That's the plan, anyway. I feel a lot better about the possibilities now that I've met Marley, and she's advising me."

"I'm glad you met her too. So, let's go over what you want to do. We're just putting an entryway between the two shops right about here?" Will indicated the spot she thought she had in mind.

Izzy nodded. "Yes, exactly. A few inches to the right, I think. I have the key to the other shop, if you want to look around there first."

"Let's go. That will help me better spot where the load bearing areas are that I need to watch out for."

Izzy found her key, and they went into the adjacent

shop, which was totally empty except for a few remaining metal shelves that were screwed into the wall.

"Why did she leave?" Will asked as they looked around the room.

"I think it was just a hobby for her and she grew tired of it. She sold bathing suits mostly and was only open for six months or so, but still had to pay rent year-round. So, when her three-year lease ended, I wasn't surprised that she decided not to renew."

"Worked out well for you."

Izzy smiled. "It did. She was a nice lady and knew I might be interested in expanding, so she gave me a heads up and I jumped on it."

"Walk me through what you need me to do here." Will was guessing mostly installing shelves.

"More shelves definitely, and I was thinking maybe put a divider in the dressing room. It's bigger than it needs to be, and two rooms would be better than one. And anything else that you would suggest."

Will nodded. "That's an easy fix. I figured you'd want more shelves. I can add a few wooden stands to the display window too, so you can use more of that space."

"I love that idea."

Will took out his measuring tape, took some measurements and determined the best spot to start the demo. When they headed back to the other side, Izzy paused at her front door.

"Do you want a coffee? I usually get one around this time and can grab one for you?"

"Actually, that sounds good. Thanks."

While she was getting the coffee, Will got to work. When Izzy returned fifteen minutes later with the coffees, she looked surprised to see that he'd already opened up the wall. He wasn't anywhere near done yet, but you could see into the other store now and it already made Izzy's shop look bigger.

He stopped to take a sip of the coffee.

"So, I should be able to get this mostly squared away today and then I can start tomorrow on the other side. That should go pretty quickly. I should be able to get it all done tomorrow."

"Thank you so much. Can I do anything to help?"

"No. Like I said, this is a simple job. And it will go quickly. Just stay back so you don't get hurt by tripping over anything. It might get messy before I'm done."

Izzy laughed. "Okay. I have my laptop with me, so I'll do some work online for a while. If you need anything, let me know."

She headed back to the register where she had a chair behind the counter and settled in with her laptop. Will turned his focus back to the project and two hours later, he was satisfied with what he'd done. He'd cut an entrance between the two stores and framed it with polished wood. It looked good, and he called Izzy over to take a look.

"What do you think?"

Izzy closed her laptop and came out from behind the counter and got her first look at what he'd done.

"Will, that looks amazing." She ran her hand over the

wood along the side of the opening. "This is beautiful wood. Thank you so much."

He smiled, relieved and happy that she was pleased with what he'd done.

"I'm glad you like it. How about I come by a little earlier tomorrow, say around one, if that works for you?"

"That's fine. What are you up to tonight, doing anything fun?" Izzy asked as Will finished putting his tools away. He stood and lifted the heavy bag.

"A few of the guys are coming over for a game of cards. Should be a good time. Are you still going out with Rick tonight?" He hated the thought of it and was hoping she'd say she had a change of heart.

But she nodded. "Yes, Mia and Sam are coming too, so it should be fun, hopefully."

Will bit his tongue. He knew that if he didn't have anything nice to say, it was best to say nothing. "Well, I will see you tomorrow, then."

"I'll walk out with you."

Izzy grabbed her purse and laptop and held the door open for him. He grabbed a big trash bag of all the materials he'd removed and put it in the trash outside the building before waving goodbye to Izzy. He watched her walk down the wharf to the condo she shared with her sister. She'd be home in just a few minutes. He hoped, not for the first time, that this date with Rick would be her last.

CHAPTER 16

"Why don't you tell him to just meet us at The Gaslight," Mia suggested when Rick texted confirming what time they were going out. "It's silly for him to come get you if we're all going to the same place, anyway."

"Good point." Izzy suspected Rick wasn't going to be happy with the suggestion, but it did make sense. And Izzy actually preferred it, too. She still had mixed feelings about going out with Rick and was glad that Mia and Sam were joining them.

She was looking forward to going to The Gaslight. It was a great date spot as the food was creative and good, with lots of small plates that were great for sharing and they often had good bands.

As usual, Izzy had a hard time deciding what to wear. Though everyone said they couldn't tell she was pregnant, it was because Izzy did a very good job of hiding it. And it was getting a lot harder because her middle seemed to be growing rapidly all of a sudden. She looked and felt extremely bloated, and her waist was non-existent.

She searched her closet for a sweater she hadn't worn in ages. It was always a little too big for her, but she'd fallen in love with it when she first saw it and bought it anyway. It always looked good, as a black oversized sweater that was well cut was always a good choice. And now, paired with a pair of deep eggplant-colored leggings and her black boots, it worked perfectly to hide her growing middle.

She walked into the living room, where Mia was hanging out with Penny. She was already dressed and ready to go. Mia looked pretty in jeans and a soft pink cashmere sweater. She looked up and smiled when she saw Izzy's outfit.

"You look amazing. I don't know how you do it. You still don't look pregnant."

Izzy laughed. "I'm running out of options to hide it, and I'm suddenly bursting out. The whole world will see soon enough. I'm guessing maybe another week or two."

"Well, you look fabulous. Are you ready to go?"

They headed out and picked Mia's boyfriend, Sam, up along the way. They went inside and said hello to Sam's girls and his mother, who was watching them for the night. They were cute, already in their pajamas and watching a movie. They came running when they saw Mia and Izzy. The girls adored Mia and were fascinated with Izzy. Sam had brought them into the store over the summer and bought sweatshirts for both girls.

"I like your shoes," Becky said.

"Those aren't shoes, they're boots," her sister said.

Izzy smiled at both girls. "Thank you. What are you girls watching? Anything good?"

"Yes, Harry Potter! Have you seen it?"

"I have, it's good."

"Girls, say goodnight. Your dad needs to go out with his friends now," his mother said.

Sam laughed. "Goodnight. I'll see you later. I don't think we'll be out too late."

"Take your time. Have fun. I'll see you when I see you."

Izzy watched the girls race back to the sofa to finish watching their movie. They were cute. She wondered if she'd have a girl that she could watch movies with and dress in cute girly clothes, or if she'd have a boy. She didn't much care either way. For the first time, she was tempted to find out what she was having. It might be fun to start shopping for baby clothes and other things.

They left Sam's house and arrived at The Gaslight in less than fifteen minutes. It was one thing Izzy loved about Nantucket—everything was so close, either within walking distance or a short drive. She did not miss the gridlock rush hour traffic in Manhattan.

Rick was waiting outside the front door of The Gaslight when they walked up. He smiled when he saw Izzy and took a step toward them, pulling her in for a hug when she reached him.

"You look beautiful," he said as she breathed him in. He was wearing the cologne she liked. The one she'd given him for his birthday earlier in the year. And the hunter green button-down shirt that she'd always told him looked so good on him.

"You're looking handsome too. You wore my favorite shirt."

He grinned. "I did. Just for you."

"Nice to see you," Mia said politely. "You remember Sam?" They'd met briefly at one of Will's cookouts.

"Nice to see you too. Both of you," he said.

A sharp gust of wind blew, tossing Izzy's hair into her face and making her shiver.

"Let's go inside, it's freezing out here." Izzy pulled open the front door and headed in. It was busy, but they were quickly seated at one of the few remaining tables, one with a good view of where the band would be playing.

When their server came with menus, they all put in their drinks order, beers for the guys, red wine for Mia and a soda with lemon for Izzy. It was funny, but as much as she usually enjoyed a glass or two of wine when she went out, she wasn't missing it as much as she'd expected.

They decided to order a bunch of appetizers, including grilled shrimp, sesame chicken bites and a few sushi items including raw tuna nachos. Izzy used to love sushi, especially spicy tuna, but the thought of it now made her stomach protest.

"You all can have the sushi. I think I'm going to get a basic burger," she said.

Mia laughed. "Good, more tuna nachos for me."

"Have you had any cravings yet?" Rick asked.

"Yes, I never used to eat much ice cream. Now I crave it every day. And it's almost always chocolate chip that I want. And red meat too, which I never ate much of before. Crazy, huh?"

"Sounds pretty good to me, actually." Rick smiled at her and Izzy felt the pull of attraction again. For a moment, it was like they were alone, sharing a moment.

Until Sam spoke. "So, everyone knows what they want then?"

They put their order in and soon after, appetizers started coming out to the table as they were ready.

Izzy was pleasantly surprised that Rick had everyone laughing throughout dinner. He was in a great mood, and she'd forgotten how charming he could be when he tried. It reminded her of when they first started dating and how they could talk forever and he always knew how to make her laugh.

When they finished dinner and Rick excused himself to use the restroom, Izzy turned to Mia and Sam. "I think things are going well, don't you?"

Mia nodded. "I didn't know what to expect, but I have to admit, he seems like he's doing well. I never knew he could be funny."

"I haven't seen that side of him in a long time. It's nice to see it again."

Rick returned a few minutes later, and they all ordered another round of drinks and both Rick and Mia ordered the dessert special, which was a warm flourless cake with a scoop of vanilla ice cream. Izzy happily shared Rick's, and it was delicious.

"Are you having fun?" he asked as they polished off the dessert.

"I am, actually."

He laughed. "You sound surprised. I'm glad we did this, Izzy. It's only going to get better from here, you'll see." He spoke softly so only she could hear, and she nodded. If things really did keep getting better, maybe there was hope for them, after all.

The band came on soon after and they stayed for both sets. The music was great and after a while, people were up dancing. Rick had never been much of a dancer, but he surprised Izzy by inviting her to dance. Mia and Sam joined them and they had a blast on the dance floor. They danced for several fast songs in a row before the music slowed a bit and Rick pulled Izzy close and they swayed to the beat. It felt good to be in his arms again, comfortable and familiar.

"When can I see you again?" Rick asked as they sat back down again. Sam and Mia were a few steps behind them.

"I don't know. What did you have in mind?" Izzy didn't hesitate this time. She was looking forward to their next night out.

"How about Thursday night?"

"I can't Thursday. I'm going to Kate's baby shower."

"Okay, Friday, then? We can go out to dinner, you pick the place."

"That sounds great. We'll see what we're in the mood for then."

"In the mood for what?" Mia asked as she and Sam sat back down.

"Just where to go for dinner Friday night. Don't forget, we have Kate's baby shower on Thursday," Izzy reminded her and also changed the subject at the same time. Her sister had an expressive face, and she didn't want her to react to Izzy agreeing to another date with Rick.

Mia just nodded. "That's right. I still need to pick up a baby gift and figure out what to make for an appetizer."

Izzy laughed. "Just do what you always do, make guacamole. Everyone loves it."

"That's true. And it's easy enough. What did you decide to make?"

"I thought I'd make rare roast beef mini-sandwiches with blue cheese mayo and crispy bacon."

"That sounds good. I don't think you've made that before for us?" Rick said.

"No, it's an experiment I tried recently that worked." Izzy grinned. "The red meat craving I mentioned earlier."

"Izzy, I totally forgot to ask you—how did the work turn out at the shop today?" Mia asked.

"Will did a great job. The two stores are connected now and the entry way looks awesome. He's finishing up the work on the other side tomorrow."

"Will is doing the work for you?" Rick sounded a bit surprised.

Izzy nodded. "Yes. He's doing me a favor and fit it in this weekend. It's a small job so won't take too long."

"I didn't realize you were still talking to him?" Rick's good mood seemed to vanish in an instant.

As she'd done so many times before, Izzy tried to diffuse the mood change. She put her hand on his arm, so he turned and looked at her. "Will is a just a good friend, of mine and Mia's. I'm lucky he agreed to help."

Rick relaxed a little. "I'd say he's the lucky one. I'll have to stop by soon and check out the changes."

"I'd give it another week or so. I have a bunch of stuff on order, but until it arrives, that room is pretty bare. I'm going to put up a room divider for now until it's fully stocked. I don't want people wandering over there, until then."

The band finished their second set a few minutes later, and they all decided to call it a night. It was almost eleven thirty and Sam didn't want to keep his mother up too late. Izzy was ready to go too, she was tired and fighting a yawn. Normally she was in bed by ten. Rick was a night owl, though.

"Now I wish I'd picked you up. We could stay out longer."

Izzy smiled. "It's okay. I'm actually fading fast. I get tired more easily now."

They paid the bill and walked out. Sam and Mia were ahead of them, and Rick waited until they were out of earshot to give Izzy a quick hug and kiss goodnight.

"I had a great time with you tonight. I'll check in end

of the week and we can make plans for Friday. Just the two of us this time, though, okay?"

Izzy smiled. She knew they needed some alone time too, for her to really find out if they had a chance to work things out.

"Sounds good. I had a fun time tonight too."

CHAPTER 17

Izzy slept late Sunday morning, finally rolling out of bed around nine thirty instead of her usual six or so. Mia was just coming in the door after taking Penny for a walk.

"Did you have coffee yet?" Izzy asked as she poured herself a cup. She'd made a whole pot, knowing she'd be going back for more.

"No, not yet. Thanks."

They flipped on the television and watched the news for a bit. After a while, Izzy asked the question she'd avoided asking the night before as they drove home. Mia hadn't brought it up, so Izzy didn't either and just wanted to drift off to sleep with happy thoughts. In her opinion, the night had gone well and Rick and Mia got along better than she'd ever seen before. Yet, Mia had stayed silent. Which was a little worrisome.

"I thought last night went pretty well. What did you think?"

Mia stirred her coffee, then took a long, slow sip. She glanced out the window at the inch or so of snow on the deck and the icicles hanging from the railing. It looked very cold.

"I'm not sure what to think, to be honest. He was definitely on his best behavior. It was interesting for me to see how charming he can be, when he tries. I've never seen that side of him before."

"I have. That's what it was like in the beginning. It was nice to see him like that again, relaxed and funny."

"I never knew he could be funny," Mia agreed. "So, what are you thinking? What do you want from him?"

Izzy sighed. "I'm not sure. In a perfect world, I'd want us to be together and him to be like this, always."

"How realistic do you think that is?"

"That's the unknown. I don't know. He swears he's a changed man and, so far, he seems to be."

"So far. How long was he like this when you first met him? When did it change?"

"About six months, I think. The first few months were a whirlwind. We fell in love so fast, and I moved in with him pretty quickly."

"At three months, right?"

Izzy nodded. "Yes. And it was good for another few months and then it changed."

"Do you have any idea why it changed? Did you guys ever talk about it?"

"He says it was work stress and financial. Rick always had a hard time getting ahead. Every time he saved a little, something would happen—his truck broke down, water heater needed replacing, expensive things that wiped out most of his savings each time."

"You don't think that's an issue now?"

"He said his new job is going really well, and he's been saving, so there's less financial stress. He also said he's been working out more too, and that helps reduce stress."

"I know you'd really love for this to work out, especially with the baby coming. But I just can't help but worry, Izzy. Please just don't rush into a decision you might regret. If you do decide to give him another chance, don't move back in with him before the baby comes. Wait, like we talked about. See how he deals with being around the baby."

Izzy took a deep breath. "You're right. I don't have to decide anything anytime soon. And in just a few months, the baby will be here. I'll see what happens then. For now, I'll just take things really slow."

Izzy stopped at the Corner Table on her way to the shop and picked up coffees for her and Will. She'd just unlocked the door and set her laptop on the counter when she heard footsteps behind her. It was Will with his bag of tools.

"Good morning! I grabbed you a coffee."

He set his bag down and pulled off his heavy work gloves before picking up the cup of steaming coffee.

"Thank you. It is cold out there today. More snow coming tonight, they say."

"Ugh. I hadn't heard that."

"Just a dusting, I think. Nothing to worry about." Will glanced at her casually. "How was your date last night? Did you guys have fun?" He looked a bit uncomfortable with the question, and Izzy felt awkward too. She'd sometimes sensed that Will might be interested in more than friendship. But the feeling was fleeting, and he'd never said anything to confirm that. She liked Will. He was a good friend and there were moments when she'd wondered about him, and he'd been wonderful when she and Rick were having problems. But once she found out she was pregnant, she'd put her focus on the baby completely.

And now that things seemed to be going well with Rick, she was only just starting to consider working on that relationship. Her feelings for Rick were complicated, and the baby was another factor that made her even more confused. Part of her felt like she should try harder to work things out, for the baby's sake, while another part wondered if a clean break might be better.

When she saw Rick, though, and danced in his arms, and spent time with him, she just wanted everything to go back to the way it was at the beginning. And he made it seem like that was possible. She wasn't sure if it was, but she was hopeful. Still, a part of her felt bad that she wasn't going to be giving Will the answer he wanted about how the night went.

She smiled. "We had fun. Food was good, and the band was too. Have you been there?"

"To The Gaslight? Yeah, a bunch of times. Caroline used to like it there." Caroline was his ex-girlfriend of almost seven years. Everyone had thought they'd get engaged—instead, they broke up and Caroline moved off-island. He'd never seemed all that upset, though, and had explained that they'd both grown apart and he was actually relieved when they broke up.

"Can I help you do anything today?" she offered.

But Will shook his head. "No, it's honestly easier if I just work alone. It shouldn't take me more than a few hours."

"Okay. Well, let me know if you change your mind, and if you need me for anything."

A look flashed across Will's face that was hard to read. He just smiled though and grabbed his tool bag. "I'll be in the other room. I might holler if I have any questions on placement for some of the shelving.

Over the next few hours, Izzy heard the noises of construction, the hammering and sawing, and now and then she saw Will go outside and return with an armful of wood. He called for her at one point, to check the placement for the shelves. While he worked, she researched what she needed to do for her website. She had a basic site already and just needed to add a store functionality.

She decided to go with Shopify and was studying how to integrate it with her site and the different vendors for her products. She wouldn't have her entire shop online, that would be too difficult to do. But she would start with her biggest sellers, the Nantucket gear and some of her specialty items. She could always keep adding more as she went along. And some unique items, she could handle the shipping herself. She was excited to get it launched soon. She and Marley had traded a few emails, and they set up a call for later in the week to discuss marketing strategies and where to advertise.

A little before five, Will called for Izzy to come see what he'd done. She walked into the other room and tears welled up immediately. She normally wasn't much of a crier, but everything seemed to make her cry these days.

"Will, it looks fantastic. Just perfect. Thank you." She walked around the room, admiring the work he'd done. The shelves were the same polished wood he'd used in the doorway and they looked lovely against all the walls. He'd divided the dressing room and added a door, so now there were two areas for customers to try things on. And the window had a pretty wooden display—a set of cubes she could use to showcase shoes, jewelry, sweaters, whatever she wished to highlight.

"I think it came out okay," he said modestly.

"Well, I'm thrilled. And I really appreciate you fitting me in so quickly. I'll be able to open this room by the end of the week. I have a ton of stuff arriving in the next few days. Let me get my checkbook and write you a check."

Izzy went back to her register, grabbed her checkbook and asked Will what she owed him. He mentioned a number that seemed far too low.

"Will that doesn't sound right. I'm sure I owe more than that?"

But he just smiled. "It's a friends and family discount. I'm happy to help and I get a deal on the wood. It didn't cost me too much. I've worked up an appetite, though. If you want, you could buy me dinner."

Izzy laughed. "Of course! Where do you want to go?"

"How about Crosswinds at the airport? It's Sunday—roast beef special. I go now and then."

"Sounds good to me."

Izzy gave him his check and followed him to his truck. Will drove to the restaurant, and they both ordered the Sunday special. Rare roast beef, mashed potatoes and gravy sounded good to Izzy too. It was comfort food, very different from how she usually ate, but now she wanted it all the time.

They chatted easily over dinner. Will was always fun to talk to, and they never ran out of things to say. Izzy was surprised by how often they seemed to finish each other's sentences and then laugh about it.

After they finished eating and were sharing a piece of apple pie, Will got a bit more serious.

"So, do you think you and Rick are getting back together?"

"I don't know. Maybe. It's too soon to know. We're going to take things slow and I'm not going to make any decisions until after the baby comes. And I see how things are then."

Will nodded. "That's smart. I'll admit that I don't like the idea of you back with him. I didn't like what I saw before you broke things off."

"He really is different now. The class helped."

"That's good to hear. I just care about you, Izzy. And I want you to be happy, and safe. I'm glad you're at least waiting until after the baby comes."

She smiled. "Thanks, Will. I promise I'm not going to do anything stupid. So, are we on for trivia this Tuesday?"

He grinned. "Of course. I wouldn't miss it."

CHAPTER 18

Izzy was looking forward to Kate's shower. She'd been to a few of her appetizer parties and it was always a good time and she was also curious to see what Kate was going to receive for gifts. She'd bought Kate cute pajamas for the babies and two picture books. Being a writer, she had a feeling that Kate might appreciate some baby books. Izzy also made herself a list of everything she thought she'd need for the baby and knew she needed to start shopping soon, to make sure she was ready when the time came.

Mia drove to Kate's and when they arrived at seven thirty, it looked like everyone else was there already. Cars lined both sides of the road and filled the driveway. Mia carried a big bag with their gifts and Izzy carried a box with their food, the guacamole and chips that Mia made and the mini roast beef sandwiches. Izzy knocked on the front door and someone called for them to come in. They stepped inside and into a room full of people who all yelled 'surprise!' Izzy looked around to see where Kate was and she was in the middle of the group, in a chair, smiling at them. She stood up and came over and gave Izzy a hug.

"They all surprised me too. I thought this was an appetizer party. Because we're due so close together, everyone thought it made sense to do a combined shower, so they told you to come a half hour later."

"Oh! Wow. I had no idea."

"I didn't either! And now I owe you a gift, too."

Izzy laughed. "I'm not worried about that."

"Do you want to set your food down? You can put it on the big table over there, there should be room."

Izzy did as instructed and then joined everyone. She still couldn't believe this was her baby shower too. It was so unexpected. And it made it all seem so real. In just a few months, her life was going to change in ways she couldn't even imagine.

The shower was so fun. There was so much food and Izzy ate just about everything, except the raw sushi rolls that someone brought. Kate made her bruschetta, which was out of this world, and Lisa brought bite-sized chunks of fresh lobster with melted lemon butter for dipping. There were dips and stuffed mushrooms and burger sliders. There were also some healthy options too, like salad and fresh veggies.

Once everyone had eaten, they opened all the gifts and Izzy was thrilled by how thoughtful everyone was and how generous. Kate received two of everything and said that she had almost everything she needed. Izzy received lots of cute outfits, baby blankets, books, a bouncy seat, and from Mia, a stroller that she knew Izzy had been eyeing.

"How did you…" Izzy began.

Mia laughed. "I had Angela bring it."

"She dropped it off yesterday," Angela said with a smile.

"Thank you so much. Everyone, thank you!" Izzy felt the tears brimming again. She glanced at Kate and saw her eyes were damp too.

Kate laughed. "It's ridiculous, isn't it? I cry at the drop of a hat now. Hormones are wild."

Izzy grinned. "I cried at a coffee commercial yesterday."

"It was a good commercial, though. I almost cried too," Mia said.

"This makes it all so real now," Kate said. "I haven't bought anything yet. Now I have so much."

"I was thinking the same thing. The next few months will go by fast. How are you feeling?"

"Good, so far. I'm taking it easy, like the doctor suggested. How about you?"

"So far, it's gone fine. I'm just hungry all the time and starting to feel big. Really big. I know I'm not showing much yet, but I think I will be soon."

Kate nodded. "Same here. I'm still trying to wrap my head around the idea that I'm having two babies. It's exciting but a little overwhelming too. I'm lucky that I can work from home." Kate took a bite of bruschetta before asking, "What will you do about work? Do you have any help at the store?"

"I have one woman, Leslie, that works part-time in the summer. She's going to work a few days a week for the first few months after I have the baby. And I'm going to hire someone else soon and get them trained so they can work the other shifts. At least until I'm able to be back in the store much."

"Could you maybe bring the baby to work with you and keep him or her behind the counter?" Kate asked.

"Yes, I think so, at least a few days a week. I'll have to see how that goes." Izzy hoped that the baby would be able to just sleep peacefully while she minded the store. But she knew she couldn't count on that, especially if she turned out to be a colicky baby—something she'd read about and was fervently hoping wouldn't be the case.

———

"I CAN'T BELIEVE YOU GUYS DID THIS," KATE SAID, looking around the living room where her mother and her friends Sue and Paige, her sisters Kristen and Abby, sister-in-law Beth, and friends, Angela and Mia were gathered. Izzy sat next to her, and Kate loved that she'd been equally surprised.

"I hope you don't mind the change in plans?" her mother said with a mischievous smile.

"Of course not. I'm impressed and I'm glad to share it with Izzy. She's a month ahead of me, but my doctor said it's not unusual to go early with twins, so we might be even closer together."

"How have you been feeling, honey?" her mom asked. Kate knew her mother worried, since she'd gone with her to the doctor.

"Much better. I'm resting up and have myself on a tighter schedule now, so I do an hour or two of writing first thing in the morning, every day. I used to put it off until the afternoons and this little change seems like it has lowered my stress levels, quite a bit."

"Oh, that's great. I'm glad to hear it, honey."

Two hours later, both Izzy and Kate yawned at the same time and everyone laughed.

"Have you been going to bed earlier too?" Izzy asked.

"Yes. I usually start fading around nine, so this is late for me."

"Me too. I used to stay up much later. I'm getting up earlier too. Everything is changing," Izzy said.

"It is, isn't it?" Kate patted her stomach. "It's still hard for me to believe there's two of them in there. I still don't feel much of anything yet."

"You will soon," Lisa said and stood, sending the signal that it was time for everyone to clear out so Kate and Izzy could get their rest. Everyone helped Izzy get her gifts out to Mia's car and when they were all gone, Kate collapsed in her favorite big chair and flipped on the television. She glanced around the room at the piles of baby gifts everywhere and felt utterly exhausted. She didn't have an ounce of energy to put anything away yet. She could do it in the morning.

"Hey there."

Kate jumped at the sound of Jack's voice and opened her eyes. Once again, she'd fallen asleep watching TV. She'd been doing that more often lately when exhaustion overcame her. She shifted in her chair and smiled.

"They threw me a surprise baby shower."

Jack laughed. "I can see that."

"Did you know?"

"A little bird may have told me. And also gave me a call when they all left. Did you have fun?"

"It was fun. And I was totally surprised."

Jack glanced around the room. "Looks like we cleaned up. Is there anything left that we need to get still?"

Kate nodded. "Yes, a few things. Not much, though. Now we just have to fit this all into their room."

"We can do that. I'll move a bunch of this stuff into their room tonight."

Kate felt her eyes grow heavy again. "Thanks, honey. I think I'm going to head to bed. I'll finish putting stuff away in the morning."

Jack gave a kiss goodnight. "I won't be long behind you."

CHAPTER 19

Three weeks later, Lisa and Marley were chatting over breakfast on a Tuesday morning. They were both heading to Eloise's shop for their weekly knitting class. Marley was already a better knitter than Lisa, who had been doing it longer. Lisa didn't really care though. She wasn't that serious about it and knew if she kept at it, she'd either improve or get bored with it again. She wasn't sure yet which way it would go.

"So, it looks like I'll hopefully have my commercial license in another week or so. Chase is almost finished and then I just have to wait for someone to come and inspect it. I called yesterday, and they said this time of year it's not too busy, so I could probably be seen pretty quickly."

"Oh, that's wonderful. I'm so happy for you," Marley said.

"Thanks. It's too bad though that by the time I'm able to serve quiche again, you'll miss it." Marley's stay was scheduled to end that Saturday. Lisa was going to miss her company. They were close in age and Marley was easy to be around.

"About that. I've been thinking. If you have the room, I'd like to extend my stay for another month or so. I'm pretty sure I'm probably going to want to buy something. I could see myself staying on Nantucket indefinitely and going back to the West Coast periodically to see my kids."

"Oh! Yes, of course. Did you live near your children?" Lisa couldn't imagine living on the other side of the country, so far away from her family. But she knew that most children didn't all live so close to where they grew up.

"Not too far. Depending on traffic, an hour or so. But they are both so busy with work and their social lives, so I don't see them all that often. We talk all the time, though and text. My son especially loves to text. To be honest. I'd probably see them just as often if I end up living here."

"Well, that's good then. I hope you will decide to buy something here. I'd love to see you stay. I'll have to introduce you to my friends Sue and Paige. You'll love them. I'll have them over for dinner one of these nights."

"That sounds fun. I'd love to meet your friends."

THEY HAD A GOOD CLASS. IT WAS A SMALLER GROUP, ONLY six students this time, which meant they got some extra attention from Eloise and Lisa was glad to see that annoying Violet and her friend weren't there. She hoped they were finished with the classes. She wouldn't miss her endless complaining. Violet wasn't picking up knitting very well. She made Lisa look accomplished.

As they were getting in the car to go home, Lisa's phone rang and it was Jack. He sounded more upset than she'd ever heard him.

"Lisa, it's Jack. I'm at the hospital with Kate. She had another episode this morning, cramps and bleeding. Fortunately, it happened just as I was about to head out for the day and I brought her right in. There was a lot of blood and she was feeling lightheaded, so her doctor said for us to go right to the ER."

"Is she okay? Are the babies okay?" Lisa tried to sound calm, but she was instantly fearful for all of them.

"They ran a bunch of tests. We're waiting for the results. But they said the babies are okay."

"I'll be right there."

"Thanks. I know she'll be glad to see you."

———

LISA TOOK A DEEP BREATH AS SHE ENDED THE CALL. "I have to drop you off and then head to the hospital. They said this could happen and hopefully, it will be fine, like it was last time." Lisa explained about Kate's condition and the bleeding.

"How scary. Anytime there's bleeding when you're pregnant, you worry."

"I know. At least Jack was with her and brought her right in."

Lisa dropped Marley off and was at the hospital five minutes later. She went straight to the ER, and they directed her to where Kate and Jack were. Kate's eyes welled up when Lisa walked up to her and gave her a big hug.

"I'm so sorry, honey. Are you feeling any better?"

Kate shook her head. "I'm still cramping and spotting a little. Not as much as before, so hopefully that might be good. The nurse said the doctor should be in soon with test results."

"Were you doing anything? Or did this just come out of nowhere?"

Kate looked at Jack and then back at her mother. "I may have overdone things a little this morning. I had a burst of energy after breakfast and decided to organize the babies' room. I was maybe lifting a little more than I should have, rearranging the closet and moving stuff around."

"I read her the riot act. It won't happen again. Right, Kate?" Jack's words were strict, but he was holding Kate's hand and Lisa could see the love in his eyes. He was worried sick about his wife.

"No. I'll be more careful."

A tall man carrying a clipboard and wearing a stethoscope around his neck came into the room.

"Kate, I have your results back. All your bloodwork came back good. There's nothing else going on here. Your babies are fine. Your cervix is still blocked, the placenta previa condition you've been told about before. But, it doesn't look any worse. You just aggravated the area, and that caused the bleeding. So, it's okay for you to head home, but please don't overdo it. Rest and relaxation. Got it?"

Kate nodded, and both she and Jack looked relieved. "Yes. I promise to take it easy. I was just feeling so good this morning. I won't make that mistake again."

"Good. It's normal to go a little early with twins, but if you can at least get to thirty-six weeks, that would be ideal. They might still be small, but they should be healthy if you get that far." He frowned. "If you don't take it easy, you run the risk of more bleeding and possibly going into very early labor, and that is not ideal."

"I understand. Thank you."

The doctor left and said the nurse would be in shortly with Kate's discharge papers.

"Thank goodness. I hope you're going to go home and stay in bed the rest of the day, at least until your cramping eases up," Lisa said.

"I can't wait to crawl into bed and just watch movies the rest of the day. I'm going to take the day off from writing."

The nurse came in with the discharge papers and they all walked out together. Lisa gave them both a hug before she left.

"Call me if you need anything, honey."

"I will. Thanks, Mom."

CHAPTER 20

I zzy was grateful that Marley decided to extend her stay on Nantucket and was still taking an interest in helping her. Her new larger store officially opened two weeks ago, when all the additional merchandise she'd ordered came in and she stocked the shelves and excitedly removed the divider between the two shops. The other side looked great, and everyone that came in was full of compliments.

But she didn't see the sales bump she was hoping for.

"Don't be discouraged," Marley said. They'd met for coffee again and were both at the Corner Table sitting side by side with their laptops open. "What are your sales normally like at this time of year? Can you look up last year's info?"

Izzy quickly pulled it up.

"Oh, that's interesting. We're actually a little ahead of last year for this month."

Marley nodded. "By how much?"

"Eighty dollars. Not much, really."

"No. But it shows this is a very slow month, and you're at least a little ahead. The store looks great. The people just aren't here yet. And there's not much you can do about that."

Izzy sipped her coffee and worried. She knew it was good to be ahead of where she was last year, but if she factored in the rent increase, she was actually behind.

"I know what you're thinking, that you're paying more in rent, so you're not really ahead?"

Izzy laughed. "Was it that obvious?"

Marley smiled. "Well, it's what I would be thinking too if I were in your shoes. But that's why we need to go where the people are. It's time to focus on driving traffic to your online store. How are sales there?"

Izzy pulled up her Shopify dashboard and was surprised by what she saw there.

"I don't understand. According to this, I sold more online yesterday than in the store and it's double what I did the day before. How could that be?"

Marley looked pleased. "That's encouraging. Did you set up the social media accounts we talked about? Maybe something was shared. That could account for a sudden spike."

Izzy nodded. "I already had an Instagram account for the store, and Facebook. I added TikTok and Pinterest and I've been putting pins up that link to the online store." She thought for a moment and grinned.

"What is it?" Marley asked.

"My friend Will stopped by the store yesterday. We

were chatting and he told me I looked cute. I was wearing some new stuff we were also selling in the store. I do that as much as possible—it helps sell the clothes when people see them on me. Anyway, he actually suggested we shoot a little video of me in the store, talking about the clothes."

"That's a great idea!"

"It was just fun and silly. We had a good time with it. I was wearing this new Nantucket sweatshirt in this gorgeous pale yellow and paired it with navy leggings that have a cool texture to them. And I was wearing these ankle boots. They're super cute and comfy too." She lifted her leg so Marley could see the camel-colored boots.

"Very cute. So what did you do with the video?"

"Uploaded it everywhere. First as an Instagram story, then repurposed it to Pinterest with a link back to the store. I have Instagram automatically set to copy to Facebook and I managed to put it on Tik Tok too." Izzy looked up each site, beginning with Instagram. There was a good response everywhere, but when she looked up Pinterest, they both dropped their jaws.

"Well, isn't that interesting? It looks like you went viral on Pinterest. Look how many people have pinned you. And look where you've been pinned."

Izzy quickly saw a running theme. "It's all pregnancy-related boards. New moms. How to look good when you're expecting."

"I think we've just uncovered a great little niche for you."

"But I'm not a pregnancy shop," Izzy protested.

"You don't have to be. But while you're pregnant

especially, you should take advantage of it and regularly shoot little videos like this with you modeling different outfits that look good. You can do by topic too—The first three months, How to hide your bump, Where did my waist go? Have fun with it."

Izzy laughed. "Where did my waist go? I love it."

"Do you have that sweater for sale in the shop, by any chance?" Marley was eyeing the classic Fisherman knit sweater that Izzy had paired with her faded blue jeans. The sweater was a gorgeous natural oatmeal shade with cabling all over. It was soft and made of all organic cotton. Izzy had seen a picture of it and fell in love instantly. It was even prettier in person, which was rare.

"I do. This just came in yesterday and I couldn't wait to wear it. It is pretty, isn't it?"

"It's gorgeous, and it screams Nantucket. When we finish here, let's go by the shop and I'll shoot a mini-video that you can post everywhere, but we're going to take it a step further and turn the post into an ad. This is the kind of thing that people go nuts over on Pinterest."

Izzy liked the idea. "I never thought much about it before, but I've bought clothes off Pinterest. It's easy to lose track of time there as you click from one photo to another."

"Exactly. What about the jeans? Do you sell those too by any chance?"

"Yes. These are my favorite pregnancy jeans so far. Just as an experiment, I ordered some for the shop. And they've been a good seller since I put them out a few weeks ago. It's hard to find this kind of thing on Nantucket."

"Excellent. We are going to have fun with this. We can actually shoot a few videos in the store, starting with this one. You can model a few other outfits and post those on different days this week. And let's make a plan for your marketing for the next few weeks. This is what I think we should do…"

Two weeks later, Will stopped by Izzy's shop to say hello. He stopped in whenever he was downtown, which was usually at least once every week or two. He'd just had lunch with a friend at Oath Pizza, which was right around the corner from Izzy's place.

The store was empty when he stepped inside, but Izzy was a whir of energy, packing a sweater into a box at the counter and he noticed that there was a stack of boxes behind her, all addressed and ready to go to the post office.

"Hey there. How's everything going? What's all this?" Will glanced at the pile of boxes behind her.

Izzy smiled as she taped up the box and took a break for a moment.

"You'd never know it by this empty store, but I'm having my best month ever. I've never been so busy. It's all the online sales. Thanks to Marley."

"Really? That's wonderful. Do you want some help to carry this to the post office?" It was just a few blocks away, and if he helped, Izzy wouldn't have to make multiple trips.

"If you have the time, that would be wonderful. This is the last one that has to go out today." Izzy printed out a label for the box and then they were ready to go. Will gathered up as many boxes as he could carry while Izzy put a sign in the window that said she'd be back in twenty minutes. She gathered the remaining boxes, and they walked over to the post office.

"Is it like this every day now?" Will asked as they walked.

"No. Some days it is, though. It depends if I'm promoting an item that my vendor can ship or something that is only available in my shop and that I have to mail out myself."

"I'm glad it's going so well. And once the weather gets better, the store sales will pick up too."

Izzy nodded. "Usually once Daffodil weekend comes, the foot traffic starts getting better each week. I'm actually kind of glad the store is slow now, so I can handle the post office runs and all the packing and shipping I've been doing lately. If it stays like this, I'm going to need to hire a dedicated person to help with this while someone else watches the store."

Will grinned. "That's a good problem to have."

"I know! I'm excited that it's off to such a good start. I really didn't anticipate this, so soon. It's all because of Marley. She's been like my retail guardian angel."

"She's still here? I thought she was only staying for a month."

"She extended her stay and is looking to buy something soon. So, hopefully I'll be picking her brain for a long time to come. I think she's going to make a business out of it—doing consulting for other retail sites. She really knows her stuff."

"That's awesome. How are you feeling? You look great." Izzy's skin was glowing and while it was finally obvious that she was pregnant, she'd only really gained weight in her stomach and Will thought she looked adorable. But that was nothing new. She always looked adorable to him, pregnant or not.

"I'm good. Really good. I'm not as tired as I used to be. I'm in a high energy phase that I hope continues."

"How much longer do you have?"

"Not quite two months. It's going fast."

Will hated asking the next question, but Izzy never mentioned Rick so he wasn't sure if he was still in the picture or not.

"How are things going with Rick?"

"Okay. We're both busy, so I haven't seen a lot of him. We usually meet for dinner or a movie once every week or so. I let him know I won't be rushing back into anything. I really need to see how things go with Rick once the baby comes. It's impossible to know for sure, until then."

Will nodded. Her answer made sense, even though it disappointed him that she was still considering a future with Rick.

"You still up for trivia tomorrow night?"

Izzy grinned. "Of course. I wouldn't miss it."

CHAPTER 21

"This is insanely good," Marley said as she took another bite of Lisa's lobster quiche. It was a Saturday morning, and she had a full house for breakfast. The inn itself was still slow, and Lisa was glad for multiple reasons that Marley had decided to extend her stay. There was no one else at the moment, though she did have several rooms rented for the coming week and people checking in later in the day.

"That's one of the best things my Mom makes. Everyone goes nuts for the lobster quiche," Kate said as she cut herself a second slice. Kristen, as usual, was just having some fruit and a toasted bagel with butter. Abby was already on her second helping, and Lisa was too. Rhett was sitting back and sipping his second cup of coffee.

"How are sales going, Mom?" Kate asked.

Lisa frowned. "Not so well, to be honest. I've called around to a few restaurants, and the only place that was interested so far is Mimi's Place. Paul said he'd be glad to try a lobster quiche for their Sunday brunch and he ordered a few key lime pies. Rhett did too."

"Once we open for brunch on Sundays in the summer, I'll add the quiche, too. It's just too slow right now."

"Oh, I know. I don't know what I expected. Of course it's slow this time of year."

"Have you given any thought to online sales? We talked about it initially as a possibility. I know you wanted to start with the local shops first," Marley said.

Lisa nodded. "I don't know much about online sales or, as it turns out, local sales either." Lisa was feeling a bit sorry for herself and wondering if she'd made a mistake adding the commercial kitchen.

"Well, I think it could potentially be a much bigger market for you. Especially if you start with this lobster quiche. It's delicious and unusual. It could be your signature item. Your only item, initially."

"You can get the lobster at a discount through Jack— the wholesale price he gives all the restaurants," Kate said.

"And lobster is a premium product. People expect to pay a higher price for it. And they expect Nantucket in general to be higher priced," Marley added.

"If you're open to it, we could work on a social media strategy for you, one that is consumer facing. That's entirely different from what you've been doing locally where it's business to business," Marley explained.

"I ran into Izzy at the post office the other day," Kristen said. "Her arms were piled high with packages that she was mailing out. She said her online sales were crazy good."

Marley smiled. "We could take a similar approach with you. And once we get you up and running, we could look into partnerships with places like Gold Belly. You need to be ready for that though—have systems in place for a higher level of production and a track record of sales and social media proof."

"Social media proof? What is that?" Lisa hadn't a clue what Marley was referring to.

"It's when people comment on your social media posts and your website, raving about your product. And once they taste it, they will."

"Oh! Okay. Well, just tell me what to do and I'll do it."

"First, we'll get the Beach Plum Cove Inn more visible on social media. We'll go deeper everywhere and post more often. Do you do that yourself now?"

Lisa shook her head. "No. Kate handles all my ads and social media."

"Okay, so let's have Kate sit in our meeting, if she can?"

Kate nodded. "I'd love to. I really enjoy the marketing stuff and would love to learn more from you about the ad stuff."

"I'm happy to help. This could serve double-duty too. You can promote the inn at the same time that you promote the lobster quiche. They reinforce each other.

People will like the idea of ordering a quiche from an actual Nantucket Inn."

"Well, I think it sounds like a great idea," Rhett said. "And with all this talk of lobster quiche, I have to go get myself a slice."

LISA AND KATE SAT DOWN WITH MARLEY THE NEXT DAY and mapped out an online marketing strategy for the lobster quiches that involved free social media posting and paid ads. The orders came in slowly at first, none at all the first day, which Lisa found discouraging, but Marley told her not to worry.

"It takes time to get things rolling. The orders will come, trust me."

And they did. Two orders the next day. Three the day after that. Then five for a few days. And then the social media proof came. The comments on the posts and ads raving about the sweet fresh lobster and creamy custard and flaky crust. And some of the first round of people ordering came back for more, sending as gifts or just more for themselves. Lisa was shocked when she opened her laptop to check incoming orders and saw that they'd doubled from the day before. She had ten quiches to make that day. A week later, the daily average doubled.

Which was wonderful, but also created a new problem. The time had come to hire someone to help. Lisa was spending more time packing and shipping the quiches than actually making them. If she could have someone else take over the packing and shipping part, she could handle what she was good it—making the quiches. She also talked to Marley about cutting back on the ads a little. She was worried that sales might increase to a level that she couldn't easily handle by herself.

"Of course, we can put the brakes on things a bit. Now that we know the ads work, we can scale them up or down pretty predictably. And even cutting back, you might still see a steady growth in sales as your social media proof continues to grow too," Marley said.

"I might know someone who could be interested," Abby said. "My friend Shannon was saying not too long ago that she'd love to find something part-time now that her kids are in school full-time. I think she'd want mother's hours, so probably afternoons and home for when the kids get out of school."

"That might work. Do you want to have her get in touch with me?"

HAVING SHANNON A FEW HOURS A DAY WAS SUCH A HUGE help. She came around one each day and worked until three, packing up the day's orders and taking them to the post office. Shannon worked as an office manager before she had her children, and she quickly took charge to organize Lisa's shipping and packaging. Because the food was perishable, it had to be packed carefully, with dry ice and shipped overnight, which was expensive, but Lisa quickly discovered that people expected it with food, so they didn't mind. Shannon worked a full day on Monday as they had double the orders to fill, as Lisa took Sundays off from baking. She needed the break.

Still, Rhett was concerned a few weeks later and insisted on taking Lisa out to dinner that Saturday night. They went to Keepers, one of their favorite restaurants and over a delicious dinner, he told her that he thought she was pushing herself too hard.

"It doesn't look like you're having enough fun with this new venture."

Lisa smiled. "The thrill has worn off just a little," she admitted. "It's great overall, though. I never expected sales to be so strong."

"Well, I'm not surprised. Your quiche is amazing and Marley is too. She's an e-commerce powerhouse. You couldn't have anyone better advising you…about generating sales. But, I worry that you might burn yourself out soon."

Lisa took a sip of her buttery chardonnay and thought about what Rhett said. The thought had crossed her mind too. Especially as they randomly had spikes in orders that were sometimes hard for her to handle. A good problem to have, but still.

"I think you need to consider hiring someone else. Someone to help you with making the quiches. Train them to do it exactly the way you do. Then you can free yourself up, if you want to take time off or take on more orders. It will give you flexibility."

"I hadn't thought about that, but you may be right. It's been wonderful having Shannon help. And I recently hired her friend, too. She's taken on the Saturday shipping and has come in a few times to help when we've had order spikes."

"I'll put the word out at the restaurant and see if anyone knows anyone. People are always looking for more work this time of year."

CHAPTER 22

Izzy's due date was exactly one week away, and she'd never felt so grumpy.

"Have I mentioned that I want this baby OUT, like now?" Izzy and Mia were sipping their morning coffee and relaxing on the living room sofa. It was a lazy Sunday morning and neither one of them had to be anywhere or do anything in particular that day.

"I thought I might make a chicken stew later. I'm kind of in the mood to cook a little and they're talking about snow again now."

"Mmm, that sounds good. Who is talking about snow? How much?"

"I don't think it's supposed to amount to much. Just a dusting. I had a notification on my phone earlier."

"Well, thankfully we don't have to worry about shoveling here."

"I know. One thing I love about living in a condo."

Izzy got up to refill her coffee and as she was standing

in the kitchen holding the pot of coffee, her water broke and puddled on the tile floor below her. She didn't realize what it was at first, as it was all new to her. But she quickly figured it out when the mild ache she'd felt earlier turned into an angry cramp.

"Mia, I think it might be time to go to the hospital."

When they arrived at the hospital, Izzy was quickly admitted and settled in a delivery room. Mia stayed with her and suggested she hold off on calling Rick until they knew for sure that the baby was coming.

"Sometimes it's a false alarm and they might send you home. I think. I don't really know either."

But it wasn't a false alarm.

"Your labor has started," the doctor, a young woman who looked almost too young to be a doctor, assured them. "We've called your doctor and she will be here soon. You're almost three centimeters dilated."

Another cramp, much stronger this time, took Izzy by surprise and she yelped from the pain. Mia grabbed her hand and squeezed. She looked up at the doctor. "Can you give her anything for the pain?"

The doctor addressed Izzy. "We can make you more comfortable, if that's what you would like. Some prefer to avoid drugs and go natural. It's entirely up to you."

"I'll take the drugs, please," Izzy said without hesitation. Her plan all along had been to try to minimize the pain as much as possible.

"I'll have the nurse come in shortly to give you something. Try to rest up."

As soon as she was out of earshot, Izzy looked at her sister. "I don't understand why anyone would willingly choose to do this naturally. I've never felt anything like this pain. And I know it's going to get worse."

"I'm with you. I don't understand it either. But they say the recovery is easier if you don't use any pain drugs. They also say it's the worst pain but the fastest to forget, or something like that."

Izzy laughed. "I'm not likely to forget what this feels like. But to each their own."

An anesthesiologist came in a few minutes later and positioned Izzy to give her the epidural shot. He had her lay on her side and round her back so he could carefully insert the catheter into her lower back and to the epidural space near the spinal cord. It didn't take long and in about twenty minutes, Izzy felt the numbing effect and the pain was dulled. She could still feel the contractions happening, but they were no longer painful.

"Do you want me to call Rick now?" Mia asked.

Izzy nodded. "I'll call him if you hand me my phone."

Rick's phone rang several times and was about to go into voice mail when he answered, his voice thick with sleep. "Izzy? Is everything ok?"

"I'm in the hospital with Mia. My water broke. They just gave me an epidural. I don't know how long it will be now, but the baby is coming."

"I'll be right there." Rick was suddenly wide awake,

and Izzy felt a wave of exhaustion as another painless cramp came and went. She closed her eyes for just a moment. And didn't open them again until she heard Rick's voice. She must have dozed off for a bit.

"Izzy, how are you feeling?" Rick nodded to Mia. "Hi, Mia."

"Hi Rick. I'm going to go get a coffee. Do either of you want one? Izzy, I'm not sure if you can have one."

"I'm good," Izzy said.

"I'd love one. I haven't had any yet."

"I'll be back in a bit." Mia left, giving Izzy and Rick some privacy for a few minutes. He sat next to her and took her hand, squeezing it gently.

"I can't believe it's almost time. What are you hoping for, a boy or a girl?"

Izzy smiled. "Just a healthy baby." Though she'd been tempted a few times to find out what she was having, she'd decided to wait. She was excited to find out, and it was something to look forward to after getting through the birth.

"Are you in any pain?" Rick asked.

She shook her head. "I was earlier, but they gave me the epidural before it got too bad."

"Good. Soon we'll be a family. And you'll move back in." He spoke surely, as though this was a fact. And somewhere, deep under her drug-induced haze, Izzy felt a hint of irritation.

"We'll see. I told Mia I would stay with her for a year after I have the baby."

"Sure, but that was before we got back together."

Izzy shot him a look, and he knew to back down.

"Right…I know we are taking it slow still. But I was thinking, what if once you're home and feeling better, if you maybe spend the weekend and we can have a taste of what it will be like to be living together as a family."

Izzy didn't hate that idea.

"That might be a good first step. We'll talk more once I'm home and feeling better."

Mia returned a few minutes later with the coffees and handed one to Rick.

"Did they say how long it will be before you start delivering?" Rick asked.

"They don't know. She needs to get to ten centimeters, and she's only at three now. It could be hours or it might go quickly. The nurse said it varies."

"Okay." Rick opened his coffee and took a sip. Izzy closed her eyes again and drifted off to a wonderful hazy place where she was half-awake. She rested there for a while until she was surprised by a contraction that ripped through her and that she felt more than she'd expected. She moaned and both Rick and Mia were immediately concerned.

"What is it, Izzy? Are you alright?" Rick asked.

"Did you feel pain?" Mia asked as a nurse walked up to them.

"I did a little. Not too bad, but it surprised me."

"We can add some medicine to your epidural," the nurse offered.

"Yes, please do." Izzy wanted to return to the hazy, happy place.

A few minutes later, more medicine was added to the epidural catheter and the nurse also checked Izzy's cervix.

"Seven centimeters dilated now. Won't be too much longer. Your doctor will be here soon to check on you."

Thirty minutes later, Izzy's doctor, Tina Powers, a tiny woman in her fifties, walked into the room. She was dressed in her doctor whites, with her shoulder-length brown hair tied back in a ponytail, making her look younger. She smiled when she saw Izzy.

"So, your baby decided to come a little early."

"Is that a bad thing?" Rick asked.

The doctor shook her head. "Not when it's only a week. Nothing to worry about. Let's take a look."

Izzy shifted as a big contraction swept through her. She was grateful for the epidural because she didn't feel any pain, just pressure, and she had a feeling they were getting closer.

"You just went to nine centimeters. We're almost ready to get this delivery started. I'll be back shortly to check on you."

She left and Izzy closed her eyes again. She was so tired. She could hear Mia and Rick chatting softly. When she opened them again, the doctor was back.

"Okay, Izzy. It's time to push. Can you do that for me?"

Izzy gathered her strength and felt the urge to push. She bore down and both Mia and Rick cheered her on.

"Izzy, you're doing great!" Mia said.

"That was good, Izzy. Do it again, please."

"Give it a good one, Izzy!" Rick encouraged her.

She pushed, and she pushed and pushed. It was exhausting. And she just wanted to go back to sleep.

"Izzy, stay focused. You're in the home stretch now. A few more big pushes."

She tried to focus and to push. Again and again. And then finally there was a huge push and then a whoosh, followed by cheers from Mia and Rick.

"That was pretty incredible," Rick said.

"Good job, mom," the doctor said as Izzy's baby took her first breath and cried. And it was the most beautiful sound Izzy had ever heard. The doctor smiled. "Congratulations, you have a healthy baby girl." She placed the baby on Izzy's chest and had Rick cut the umbilical cord.

Izzy looked down at the tiny face and snuggled the baby close to her.

"Emily. Her name is Emily."

"It's wonderful to meet you, Emily." Mia had tears in her eyes and Rick did too.

"Emily is a good name," Rick said.

One of the nurses come over after a short while. "Let's take Emily and get her settled so Izzy can get some rest. Sound good?"

Izzy nodded. She was reluctant to let go of the baby, but it was so difficult to keep her eyes open.

"Izzy, I'll stop by later tonight," Mia said.

"I'll call and maybe come by later too."

Rick gave her a quick kiss goodbye, and Izzy floated away soon after.

MIA CAME THE NEXT DAY TO BRING IZZY HOME. RICK HAD offered to help, too, but Izzy was still so tired. She told him it was easier for Mia to do it and that she'd call him later.

Her first week home with the baby was a blur. It was wonderful and exhausting at the same time. She knew she was lucky with Emily as she seemed as though she was going to be a good baby, not colicky like Izzy had heard some babies could be. She was grateful for that. Emily definitely cried when she needed something, but she was easily soothed and she liked to sleep.

Rick came by a few times that week to visit. He seemed in awe of the baby. Especially when he held her, and she cooed up at him. He said that she was the most beautiful baby he'd ever seen. And Izzy had to agree with him there. She thought Emily was just perfect, with her baby fuzz for hair and her pink skin and little rolls of baby fat around her knees. She had a quizzical expression at times that cracked Izzy up, and she wondered what was going through her daughter's mind.

After about two weeks, Izzy started to feel semi-normal and a bit stir-crazy to get back in the shop. She had it well-covered. The girls gave her daily updates and she could see the sales coming in through the website, but she missed the energy of being in the thick of it.

So, on the Monday of week three, she packed Emily into her baby carrier along with several baby blankets, plenty of diapers, bottles, and formula. They went into the shop and Izzy grew teary-eyed when she saw what was behind the counter.

Will had stopped by to visit a few times since she'd been home from the hospital and like everyone, he adored Emily as soon as he met her. Izzy had told him that she was planning to go back to the store soon and wanted to bring Emily along with her. The girls told her that Will had dropped off a surprise at the store, but that they couldn't tell her more than that. Will had made them promise to keep quiet.

He'd built her a wooden stand behind the counter that she could set the baby carrier into or if she wanted, she could take Emily out of the carrier and place her in the stand itself as it was like a big bowl with high sides all around. Izzy set the carrier in the stand and it fit perfectly. She positioned the carrier so Emily was facing her and she could keep an eye on her as she worked. She called Will immediately to thank him.

"Will, this is so nice of you. Thank you. Emily and I both love it."

"I'm glad. It was a fun project for me. Maybe I'll pop in today or tomorrow to see how she likes it."

"Of course, come in anytime."

Izzy was still smiling as she hung up the phone and opened her laptop. She checked her sales and smiled again. The store was still slow, but her online sales were steadily increasing each week. While she'd been home and not working for the past two weeks, her total sales were actually up. It was an amazing thing. The morning flew as she worked. A few customers came in, but most of her work was done online while Emily slept peacefully beside her. She woke a few times to eat or to have her diaper changed and usually fell right back asleep again.

She woke totally around noon and didn't seem to need anything. She just lay there happily cooing and looking around with her eyes wide. Izzy had noticed that she seemed to respond to bright colors. She held up a new sweater that was bright blue and Emily's face lit up. A moment later, Will walked through the door.

"Hey there!"

Will walked over to Emily and smiled at her.

"She is so cute. And she looks great in the stand."

"It's working out perfectly. I can sit here and work and keep an eye on her easily."

"Are you hungry? I just grabbed a few slices of pizza from Oath. Thought you might want to share."

Izzy's stomach rumbled. "What kind did you get?"

"The David of course."

"Yes, please." The David was one of their special pizzas with balsamic, mozzarella and ricotta cheeses, Italian sausage, mushrooms and fresh basil. It was beyond delicious. Will had picked up two slices for each of them.

"I'm having trivia withdrawals," Will said. "I don't suppose you'll be able to do that for a while?"

"Actually, not this coming week, but the week after, Sam said his mother would love to watch Emily. She babysits his girls when we go to trivia anyway, and Sam said the girls are excited about it too." It had crossed her mind, briefly, to ask Rick to watch Emily, but that didn't feel right if it was so she could go out with her friends—especially Will, who Rick always seemed a little threatened by even though she'd assured him many times that they were just friends.

Just as Will was saying how cute Emily was again, she started to cry, the familiar cry by now that meant she had a wet diaper. Izzy took her into her bathroom, threw out the dirty diaper and wrapped her in a fresh one. When she came back to the register, Will was watching them and had a funny look on his face.

"She looks so peaceful now, and happy."

"I'd be happy too if someone took my wet diaper away." Izzy laughed. "Do you want to hold her?"

"Could I?" He looked a bit nervous and excited at the same time.

Izzy handed her to him and showed him how to gently hold her so that her head stayed supported. Will seemed in awe as he looked down at her and Emily stared up at him, her eyes wide. He was wearing a bright red sweater and Emily kept her eyes focused on it.

"I think she likes your sweater. She likes vibrant colors."

"Just like her mom. Maybe she'll go into fashion too." Will handed Emily back, and Izzy settled her into her carrier. After a moment, Emily's eyes shut, and she was fast asleep.

"She seems really good," Will commented.

"So far, she is. I'm lucky."

"Is it hard? Doing it all by yourself?"

"It's a lot, but I'm not really by myself. I have Mia and Rick and you, and I have help in the store. The girls have been great and that has given me flexibility to work from home or to not work at all."

"It sounds like a lot. But you're handling it exactly how I knew you would. You're going to be a great mom, Izzy."

"Thank you." Her eyes watered, and she laughed. "Silly hormones. I'm still crying at everything."

Will stood and pulled her into a hug, holding her tight for a moment before letting her go.

"What was that for?"

He smiled. "You just looked like you really needed a hug. And I wanted to hug you. I should probably head back to work. I have to be at a client site in Siasconset in twenty minutes."

"You'd better hurry then. Thanks, Will. For everything."

"It was my pleasure. If you need anything, give me a holler."

Emily woke as Will stood to leave, and both she and Izzy watched as he walked out the door.

"That's a good man, Emily. Someday, I hope you meet someone like him."

CHAPTER 23

Kate felt monstrously huge. She hadn't actually gained that much weight, a total of forty-five pounds. But, for someone that was always slim, it felt uncomfortable, especially as one of the babies seemed to have the hiccups all the time. The doctor said it might have something to do with their positions. One was wedged straight across the top and when she had hiccups, Kate's stomach moved in rhythm.

The doctor had told her the baby on top was the girl. Kate was still debating which name to go with. Emily had been high at the top of her list, but Izzy named her baby Emily so she didn't want to be a copycat or cause confusion as they were friends, and Kate hoped that her babies would eventually have playdates with Emily. She'd grown closer to Izzy too, in recent months. She'd always been friends with Mia, but now she and Izzy had a lot in common and it was nice to have someone to talk to that was going through the same thing she was.

Kate had made it past the danger point. Her doctor wanted her to at least get to thirty-six weeks, so the babies would be big enough that they shouldn't have the complications that premature babies often did. And since her last scare, she'd been very careful to not push herself too much and to make sure she was getting plenty of rest. She'd been mostly living in her bed for the past few months, lounging there most of the day, and writing in bed. She propped herself up with a pile of pillows and was surprised by how productive she could be there. And when she felt like napping, she just shut her eyes and drifted away for a while.

Today was her week thirty-seven check-up and she was heading to her doctor's office in a few minutes. She used the bathroom before she left and noticed a tiny spot of blood on the tissue. And on the short drive to the doctor's office she felt a cramp, stronger than the ones she'd felt before, and she picked up her speed, feeling suddenly nervous and anxious.

Her doctor smiled when she entered the exam room and when Kate filled her in on the spotting and cramp, she checked Kate out quickly, examining her cervix and doing an ultrasound.

"It's not clear if you are going into early labor or if this is another placenta previa episode. Usually that resolves by this point, but where you had some spotting, it could be that and at this point, we don't want that to go any further. I think it's time to get you into the hospital and do a c-section immediately to get those babies out before there's any distress. Can you call your husband to come and get you? I'll call ahead to the hospital and I'll meet you there shortly."

Kate called Jack, and he said he'd leave immediately.

"My car is here."

"We'll worry about that later."

Less than ten minutes later Jack arrived, and Kate left with him for the hospital. It was right around the corner from the doctor's office, and they were expecting her so she was admitted right away. She was brought to a delivery room and prepped for surgery. Jack called her mother, who said she'd call the rest of the family and they'd all be there shortly.

Everything went quickly after that. Because they were going right into surgery, Kate didn't get to see anyone before they went in. Jack was with her, after scrubbing up and donning a protective paper covering over his clothes. She was given anesthesia in her spinal area and soon after, felt pretty much numb from the waist down. She was reassured when her doctor walked into the room and smiled.

"Okay, Kate. Are we ready to do this? Let's meet your babies."

It went so quickly—more quickly than Kate expected. She was used to the stories of long labors, hours of contractions and pushing. This was nothing like that. The doctor made an incision in her abdomen and it just felt like pressure, no pain. And soon after, she reached in and lifted out the first baby, and let Jack cut the umbilical cord. The first one was the girl, and the doctor handed her to a nurse who cleaned her and wrapped her in a blanket. Less than a minute later, the doctor held up the second baby, their boy, and Jack proudly cut the umbilical cord again.

While the doctor finished with Kate, making sure everything was as it should be and then sewing her incision, the nurses placed the two babies in Kate's arms. They were laying across her chest and both Kate and Jack stared at them in amazement. It was crazy to think just moments ago these two little people had been inside of her. As she looked at their tiny faces, all pink and wrinkly and perfect, she turned her eyes to Jack.

"We did this," she said proudly. Jack was wearing a permanent grin as he looked at his family.

"We did." They'd been torn between a few names, but as Kate looked at her children, the names they were meant to have seemed clear.

"I'm thinking Annabella and Tobias. What do you think?"

Jack nodded. "He looks like a Toby to me, and that's the prettiest Annabella I've ever seen."

Kate was wheeled back to her room and soon after, the doctor went to the waiting room and let Kate's anxious family know that Kate was resting, the babies were healthy and everyone was fine. She said they could take their turns going in to see her, but that everyone should keep their visits short so Kate could get some rest.

Kate's mom and Rhett were the first to visit. Happy tears streamed down her mother's face when she saw Kate propped up in bed, holding the babies, with Jack by her side.

"Oh, Kate, they're beautiful."

"Congratulations to both of you," Rhett added.

"How are you feeling?" her mother asked.

Kate smiled. "I'm just tired. I'm still numbed up so I'm not sore, yet."

"The doctor said you'll be going home day after tomorrow. I'll stop by later that afternoon—I'll call first, of course. But I'll drop off some food for you and Jack. Maybe a lasagna or something easy you can just heat up. You're not going to feel like cooking for a while."

"Thanks, Mom. I appreciate that." And she was right. Kate knew she was going to have her hands full and there would be little time to cook, or even eat.

Her sisters and then her brother and his wife came in next and everyone offered their congratulations. Kristen and Abby also said they'd bring some food by in the next few days and would coordinate with their mother on what she needed.

When everyone except Jack left, Kate suddenly felt exhausted and ready for a nap. A nurse came and took the babies away, and Kate closed her eyes. Jack still sat beside her, holding her hand until she fell asleep. When she woke, hours later, he was still there in the chair next to her bed, sound asleep. She sighed with contentment and drifted back to sleep.

JACK WENT HOME LATE THAT NIGHT AND WAS BACK FIRST thing in the morning with two baby carriers. They kept

Kate until late that afternoon, wanting to make sure she didn't have any complications before sending her home. She was sore now that the anesthesia had worn off, and even though the incision wasn't big, it was straight across her abdomen and cut through all the muscles used daily for almost every movement. It hurt every time she got up or moved around at all. They gave her something for the pain, but it made her groggy, so she just switched to Advil, which took the edge off. And a day later, it felt more like a stiff muscle than actual sharp pains.

"I feel like a little old lady, moving around so slow," Kate made fun of herself as she got up from the sofa the next day and made her way into the kitchen. She was very grateful that her mother and sisters had all dropped off food, pasta she could heat up and rotisserie chicken she could slice and eat and as a special treat, a lobster quiche.

And Jack had been wonderful. He helped so much the first few days when Kate felt like her legs were stuck in molasses and everything she did was in slow motion. She started to feel more like herself by day four and that's when Jack went back to work and she had the babies all to herself. It was wonderful and overwhelming at the same time. She'd been warned it would be like that, though. She'd read all the books on having twins and how challenging the first year would be.

The hardest thing was that they were two entirely different people and didn't always follow the same schedule. One would fall asleep as the other was waking up and started screaming. They screamed a lot, and at first it alarmed Kate until she began to recognize the different sounds of their cries. The hungry cry versus the diaper needs changing cry and the 'I'm a baby and bored' cry.

As the first few weeks turned into a month, it got a little easier in some ways and harder in others. The hardest thing was the sleep deprivation. Kate wondered if she'd ever be able to get a good night's sleep again. She was a much lighter sleeper than Jack. And since he was the one with a set schedule, who had to get up and go to work every morning at a certain time, she tended to be the one that flew out of bed when one of the babies cried in the middle of the night.

"You need to let me get up with them sometimes. You look exhausted," Jack said one morning as Kate sipped her coffee and almost wished she could inject it into her veins to wake up faster. She was exhausted, and she knew she looked awful. A month of horrible sleep found her with dry, pale skin and dark hollows under her eyes.

"I might let you get up with them tonight. But you might be sorry you offered," she said with a laugh.

True to his word, Jack did get up. Kate heard one of them cry a little after one and resisted the urge to jump out of bed. She rolled over instead and snuggled into her pillow, trying to block out the sound. But it was pulling at her and just as she was about to give up and go to the baby, Jack spoke. "Stay in bed. I've got it." And he did. He went and gave the baby a bottle and was back in bed twenty minutes later, as Kate was almost asleep and falling fast. For the first time in weeks, she fell fully asleep and woke hours later feeling refreshed.

CHAPTER 24

"I have my first official client," Marley said at breakfast one morning. Lisa looked at her in surprise. "That's wonderful. Who is it? Someone from your California network?"

"No, though a few people have reached out to set up calls, which is encouraging. They saw my updated LinkedIn profile and checked out my website. She grinned. "You and Izzy are both case studies on my site, and I think that is how this new client found me. He's a friend of Eloise's from the knitting shop and when he told her what he was looking to do, she mentioned me. He looked up my website and I think you and Izzy closed the sale."

"Oh, good! So, who is it?"

"Mark Andrews. He's a local photographer, and he's looking to update his website and see if he can sell more of his photos, for commercial use."

"You mean like for book covers, things like that?" Lisa knew that Kate often bought photos to use for her book covers and her designers worked their magic, adding other elements like text.

"Yes, and anything, really. I met him for coffee yesterday to chat about what he's looking to do, and I think it might be a fun project. Do you know him?"

"I don't know him, but I think I've seen him out and about at local art events, like at some of the galleries Kristen works with. He's about our age, right? Year-round Nantucket resident?"

"Yes. He's a native Nantucketer. Born and raised here. He left for college and lived in the Boston area for years, but when his wife died, he moved home to Nantucket. He has two adult boys about the age of your children."

"I didn't know that about his wife. That's sad."

"It is. I think it's been hard for him, but it's been almost ten years now."

Lisa was quiet for a moment, then asked, "Is he good-looking?" She thought she knew the answer based on how much Marley was chatting about him.

"He is actually, and very nice too. Not that I'm looking for anything romantic. I'm not. Not yet. I just really enjoyed his company. It's going to be fun working with him."

"Well, that's how the best relationships start I've always found. Friends first. That's how it was with Rhett."

"It seems like the two of you are so well suited," Marley agreed. "Like you've been together for ever."

"When you get to be our age, it doesn't take as long to figure out how you feel about someone. In some ways, it's easier."

"I suppose. I never was a fan of dating. I always thought it as stressful. First dates, that is. It's almost like a job interview when you're so careful to say the right thing." Marley shuddered. "I'm in no rush for that."

Lisa laughed. "I don't blame you. I'm happy about your new client. If nothing else, you'll make a new friend."

"That's what I figured. I have more news too. I think I found a house that I'm going to make an offer on."

"You did? That's great. Tell me about it."

"It's about a mile and a half from here, on the water, but it's not one of those showy mansions. It's an older, renovated cottage. Just three bedrooms, so not too big. My favorite feature is a big farmer's porch overlooking the ocean. I can already see myself sitting there reading a book or knitting as I watch the sun set."

"That sounds lovely."

"I fell in love with it immediately. I didn't want to be too impulsive, though. I've been poking around online checking out the street and property history and there's no red flags. So, I'm going to call my realtor shortly and put an offer in."

"Good luck!"

"MARLEY BOUGHT A HOUSE TODAY," LISA TOLD RHETT AT dinner that night. They were sitting in the kitchen in their usual spots at the island, enjoying a glass of red wine and snacking on some cheese and crackers. Lisa had a roast chicken in the oven with some baked potatoes and a tossed salad. They were back to trying to eat better.

"She did? On Nantucket?"

Lisa nodded. "Yes. It sounds adorable. An older cottage on the ocean. She's paying cash, so they will be able to close in a few weeks as soon as they do a title search. I'll miss having her here."

Rhett smiled. "You miss everyone when they go away."

It was true. They'd had several guests that Lisa had grown close to and missed when they checked out and moved on with their lives. But some of them, Angela and Mia, didn't go far, and Lisa still saw them, as both girls were friends with her children.

"Fortunately, Nantucket is a small place, so I'm sure I will still see Marley too. I told her I wanted to introduce her to Sue and Paige. Maybe I'll set a dinner up this week. We've been trying to get together for a while."

"What are you up to tomorrow?" Rhett asked.

"Baking in the morning and then later in the afternoon, around four or so, I thought I'd bring some food over to Kate's."

"You just want to see those grandbabies."

"I do. I might offer to babysit for them this weekend too, either Friday or Saturday night. I think Kate could use a break and a date night would be fun for them."

"I'm sure she'd love it."

Lisa made a big pot of chicken soup with the leftover roasted chicken and brought it to Kate's the next afternoon. Kate seemed happy but exhausted, and Lisa noticed that she was looking awfully thin. Kate was naturally slim, but she'd lost all her baby weight plus an extra ten or so pounds and had a gaunt look to her.

"Honey, I'm worried about you. You need to make sure that you eat right."

"I am eating. But I'm just so busy. These two keep me running. Look at my arms, though. They've never looked so good. Look at the definition."

She pushed her long sleeves back and her arms did look good, toned and her muscles were well defined.

"Have you been working out?"

"Nope. It's just from carrying these two around, one on each hip. They are my free weights."

Lisa smiled at the image. "How's it going at night? Are you getting enough sleep?"

"What is sleep?" Kate laughed. "No, I'm not. Jack wants me to wake him up more, but I always wake up first and it's just easier for me to get up."

"You really should let him do it more. I did it most of the time with your father, but it was just too much and we ended up working out a schedule where he did it one or two night a week and that at least gave me a break. It really does get better after the first year. I promise."

"Maybe I'll talk to Jack and see if something like that could work. Thanks for the suggestion."

"Of course. Now, where are those babies? Grammy needs a snuggle."

CHAPTER 25

"**A**re you sure you're ready for this? You don't have to stay all weekend. Why not start with one night? Or you could even give him Emily for the night and see how he does by himself. That would give you a break." Mia and Penny were both in Izzy's room watching her pack for her weekend at Rick's.

"We've been talking about this for a while. We both think it's a good idea. He wants me to move back in. This is a good compromise, a way to dip my toes in the water first before diving in. It will be good for both of us, to see if this will work."

"Well, I still don't like it. But I've never liked the idea of you getting back with Rick, either."

"I know you don't." Her sister was nothing if not consistent. Izzy knew it just came from a place of love and worry for her.

"It will be fine."

"Well, if it's not fine, come home. Don't feel like you have to stay the whole weekend, okay?"

"Okay, Mom," Izzy teased her.

"I just care about you, Izzy."

Izzy gave her a hug. "I know you do. I was just teasing. Emily and I will be back before you know it."

RICK'S TRUCK WAS IN THE DRIVEWAY, BUT HE DIDN'T answer the door right away when Izzy rang. She stood there for several moments, freezing. It was cold and windy and the air was raw as it whipped into her. She set Emily's carrier down and banged on the door. Where the heck was he? She'd talked to him on the phone just an hour ago, and he'd said he had dinner in the oven and was making one of her favorite meals.

She rang the doorbell again and banged one last time for good measure. Finally, Rick came to the door, rubbing his eyes and apologizing.

"I'm sorry, I must have dozed off. I was watching TV in the other room."

Izzy stepped inside with Emily and Rick grabbed her overnight bag and shut the door behind them.

"What's that smell?" It smelled like something was either burning or very close to it.

"Oh, crap." Rick ran to the kitchen where a thin trail of smoke was coming from the oven. He clicked on the vent fan and opened the oven. A gust of smoke rushed out and Izzy saw the remains of what had been dinner.

"I'm so sorry. This was your favorite chicken, the marinated breasts from the market. I must have been out for longer than I realized."

She looked at him with concern. "Not a big deal. We can just order pizza or something. Is everything okay, Rick?"

He ran a hand through his hair and sighed. "Yeah, it's fine. Just a rough day at work. My buddy Dave lost a big job we were all counting on, so my hours might be cut for the next few weeks. We went to the pub for lunch and there was no more work rest of the day, so I had a few drinks with the guys. You know how it is."

She did know how it was. She'd seen this before. Rick and his buddies drowning their sorrows in beer and then Rick passing out on the living room sofa. She'd hoped that Rick was in the past.

"It's not a big deal, Izzy. Don't go freaking out on me. It's not going to be like it was before. I promised you that."

"I know you did. So, should we order some pizza?"

They discussed their pizza options and then Rick called the order in for delivery. Rick offered to go get it, but she didn't think that was a good idea, and she didn't want to go out and leave Emily or take her out in the cold again.

Izzy got Emily settled, changed her diaper, fed her and played with her for a bit before she fell asleep on her favorite baby blanket. She got her playpen out of the car, set it up in the corner of the room and carefully set Emily and her blanket in it. Emily stirred for a moment and then fell fast asleep.

Their pizza arrived a short time later, and they ate it while they watched a movie on Netflix. Rick was quieter than usual, and they mostly ate in silence. Halfway through the movie, she looked over and saw that he was fast asleep again.

She got up and cleared their paper plates away, and when she did, she noticed an empty beer can next to Rick's chair. She picked that up too and tossed it in the garbage. So, Rick had come home from the pub and after putting their dinner in the oven, sat down and had another drink. No wonder he fell fast asleep and almost didn't hear her banging on the front door. It was certainly disappointing, and not the evening she'd hoped for.

She checked on Emily, then set up the baby monitor in her playpen and went into Rick's guest bedroom and climbed into bed. She didn't even wake him up. He could get himself to bed.

Izzy was up early the next morning after getting up twice during the night as well, as soon as she heard the sounds of Emily moving around through the baby monitor. She changed and fed her, and while she was happily hanging out in the playpen, Izzy made herself a cup of dark roast coffee. She looked around in Rick's refrigerator, which was surprisingly bare except for a few six packs of beer, ketchup and a package of expired bacon. He never was much of a cook. She decided to heat up one of the leftover slices of pizza in the toaster oven.

She was done with her pizza and on her second cup of coffee when Rick stumbled into the kitchen, all bleary-eyed. She guessed he was nursing a painful hangover.

"Coffee?" She offered to make it for him.

"I'll do it, thanks." He made himself a cup and joined her at the kitchen table.

"So, last night didn't exactly go as planned," he said.

"No. I've burned dinner before, though. The pizza was good." But she knew he wasn't just talking about dinner, and she wasn't sure she was ready for this conversation. Because it kind of was a big deal. Especially if this was going to be typical behavior.

"I haven't done anything like this in ages. It's not who I am anymore. I swear it." He seemed genuinely contrite, and once again, she wanted to give him the benefit of the doubt.

"Good. Well, we'll just have a good rest of the weekend, then. And I'll give you some lessons on diaper changing and bottle feeding."

He smiled. "Sounds good. What do you feel like doing today and tonight?"

"I don't know. Any thoughts?" Normally, if she was home, Izzy would have plenty to do. She'd probably work a little online, go into the store for a few hours and do something with Mia in the afternoon or evening, depending on if she had plans with Sam or not.

"Well, I'd say we could go downtown and see what's going on, but it's freezing out. So not a good day for walking around. There's not much here to eat, so I could run to the store and pick up some stuff for lunch, cold cuts or whatever. And maybe if you want, we could go out to dinner tonight somewhere?"

Izzy glanced over at Emily, who was now sleeping peacefully in her playpen.

"I'd love to go out to dinner, but we have Emily. I haven't taken her to a restaurant yet. She might be fine though."

Rick grinned. "We could see what happens."

They agreed to go to Mimi's Place and to go early, before it got too crowded, in case Emily was difficult, so they wouldn't disturb too many people.

After Rick showered, he ran to the store while Izzy worked online for a bit. She was amazed by how many orders came in each day. Marley's trick with the Insta-gram videos was working well and anything that she wanted to move out of the shop, she just did a video on. She was having to place new orders more than she'd ever anticipated to keep up with the demand. Fortunately, the biggest percentage of orders came through Shopify and her partner vendors, so she didn't have to deal with packing and shipping those items.

Once Rick returned from the store and they made sandwiches for lunch, Izzy closed her laptop and curled up on the sofa with Rick and Emily to watch a few movies. Emily was good all day but didn't sleep a lot, which made Izzy a little apprehensive about taking her out to a restaurant. But she was also curious to see how she'd do and Izzy missed going out to eat. A nice glass of wine and someone else cooking and serving dinner sounded wonderful to her.

After the second movie Emily started to cry, and Izzy changed and fed her and soon she was sound asleep. While she slept, Izzy jumped in the shower and got ready to go to dinner. Emily was still sound asleep when they were about ready to go, and Izzy gently gathered her up and strapped her in her carrier. She tucked her favorite blanket around her snugly and grabbed a pacifier and a bottle in case she needed them.

Rick drove, and they arrived at Mimi's Place a little before five. Izzy knew one of the owners, Mandy, who was at the front desk when she walked in. Mandy walked over to get a good look at Emily.

"Izzy, she's so beautiful! I'd heard both you and Kate had your babies around the same time. I haven't seen hers yet either. Though with twins, I don't imagine she'll be coming to dinner anytime soon."

Izzy laughed. "This is actually our first time out with Emily too. And I'm not sure how she'll do. You might want to seat us away from other people, just in case. And don't be surprised if we have to make a quick get-away."

"I understand."

"We're not going to have to leave. Emily will be fine," Rick said.

"I know exactly where to put you. Follow me." Mandy led them to a corner table by the window. It was on the opposite side of the dining room, as far from the rest of the crowd as possible.

"I don't know how long you'll have this area to yourself, but we'll try to keep people away for as long as we can," Mandy said.

"Thank you. I really appreciate it."

Rick looked at her funny as Mandy walked away. "You don't seem very optimistic. What do you expect her to do? Look how sweet and peaceful she is."

Izzy glanced at Emily in her carrier, and she really did look angelic. Izzy wondered if she was overreacting and anticipating the worst.

"You're right. Let's order some cocktails and relax."

When their server, Stacey, came to the table, Rick ordered a draft beer and Izzy went with a glass of La Crema chardonnay. It was her special occasion chardonnay, rich and buttery and she felt like she deserved it.

When Stacey returned with their drinks, she told them the specials and they both went with the same special, blackened swordfish over lobster and corn risotto with a mango salsa. They also ordered a shrimp cocktail to share as an appetizer. Everything was delicious, and Izzy finally relaxed and ordered a second glass of wine when their swordfish arrived. Emily was still sleeping peacefully, which almost seemed like a miracle. They were having a wonderful, relaxing night out.

Until dessert came, and Emily woke up.

The screams that came from her child were like nothing Izzy had heard before. It was like the wet, hungry, bored cry all in one with an addition of extreme annoyance at being somewhere new and scary.

Izzy scooped her up, and she quieted a little. "I'm going to run into the bathroom with her and see if she needs changing or a bottle or whatever. I'll be back in a few minutes."

Rick didn't look overly concerned. "Take your time. I'll be here."

Izzy made her way to the bathroom and checked Emily's diaper. It was dry. She tried to give her a bottle, and Emily swatted it away.

"What is it then, honey?" Izzy looked at her tiny daughter and wished Emily could just tell her what the problem was. Emily just shook and scrunched up her little face, which was now very red and let out a howl. Emily looked in her purse for the pacifier and realized it was in her carrier, which was back at the table. Izzy needed to calm her down first before walking back through the dining room. She tried the bottle again and this time, Emily took it for a moment or two before pushing it away and starting to cry again.

"Okay, looks like it's time to go home." That quieted Emily. Izzy walked quickly back to the table where Rick was taking his first bite of cheesecake. He'd ordered one for her, too. But Izzy knew there was no way they were going to be able to enjoy that cheesecake in the restaurant.

"Rick, we need to get the check and go. We can pack up these desserts and finish them at home."

Rick raised his eyebrows at her like she was out of her mind.

"Why? She's a little angel again. Just put her in the carrier and enjoy your cheesecake. We'll head home after that."

"Rick, I really don't think that's a good idea." Emily was watching them both, with wide eyes and Izzy knew in her bones that it was the calm before the storm. But she also knew the look on Rick's face—when he got stubborn and dug his heels in about something. They weren't going to be leaving until he finished his cheesecake or until he experienced the less angelic side of Emily.

"Okay. But don't say I didn't warn you." Izzy buckled Emily into her carrier and when she caught Stacey's eye she waved her over and asked for the check and two to-go boxes. Rick looked irritated by the request but didn't say anything. He just kept eating his cheesecake. So, Izzy decided she might as well do the same. It did look like good cheesecake. She always liked it best when it was topped with cherries.

She took her first bite and was reaching for her second when Stacey returned to the table with the check and two boxes. A moment later, Emily discovered her vocal chords again and let out a piercing howl that seemed to echo in the room. Two tables turned to look at them. Rick continued eating his cheesecake. He made no movement toward his wallet, so Izzy reached into her purse, got out her Nantucket Threads American Express card and gave the bill and card to Stacey the next time she walked by.

"You didn't have to get dinner," Rick said as Emily belted out another scream and more tables turned their way.

"I'm happy to do it." Izzy signed the charge slip as soon as Stacey dropped it off. Izzy dumped the rest of her cheesecake in a box, and stood. She glanced at Rick's plate, which still had half a cheesecake left. "Finish that quick or take it to go. We need to leave, now. People are staring and this is embarrassing."

Rick sighed and put the rest of his dessert in the other box and followed Izzy out. She was already to the front hostess desk and said an apologetic goodbye to Mandy.

"I'm so sorry if she disturbed anyone."

But Mandy just laughed. "Please don't worry about it. I hope you enjoyed your dinner?"

"It was wonderful. And a treat to get out, even if it was a little stressful worrying about whether she would start crying again."

"Babies cry. It's what they do. I'm glad you came in."

Izzy relaxed once they were in the truck and as soon as they pulled out of the parking lot, Emily was quiet again. The motion of the vehicle rocked her to sleep. When they got back to Rick's place, he carried Emily's carrier in and Izzy grabbed the boxes of cheesecake. Emily was still sound asleep, so Izzy put her in the playpen and then settled on the sofa with her cheesecake. Rick took his to the refrigerator.

"You're not going to finish yours?"

"No, I'm going to have a beer instead. Do you want one? I'm sorry I don't have any wine to offer you. I should have picked some up. I didn't think of it when I was at the store."

"No, I'm fine. I had two glasses at the restaurant."

Rick sat next to her on the sofa and put his arm around her. She snuggled into him as she finished eating her dessert. They were halfway through a movie when Izzy heard a snore and realized Rick had fallen asleep. She took the empty beer can from his hand and threw it out along with her to-go box. Just as she was settling back on the sofa, Emily woke up and started screaming like Izzy had never heard her scream before. It was louder and more alarming even than at the restaurant.

She went to her and immediately checked her diaper, which was still dry. She took a bottle for a few minutes only, pushing it away and starting to cry again. It was too late to call anyone for advice. Rick somehow was still asleep as Emily continued to howl. Izzy pulled up her laptop and searched google for answers. But it turned out there were a million different reasons why babies cried. She tried burping her, and that didn't help. She wasn't especially hot, so Izzy didn't think she was sick. But she'd never cried like this before, and it was scary. Izzy didn't know what to do, and she was beginning to worry that something might be really wrong.

Rick woke up and stared at the two of them.

"What the…What's wrong with her?"

"Nothing is wrong with her!" And then Izzy burst into tears, too. "I don't know what's wrong with her. I've tried everything. She doesn't want food. She doesn't need her diaper changed. She's not hot, so I don't think she's sick. But, I don't know. Maybe something is wrong."

"Maybe she's just in a bad mood." Rick tried to joke about it. "Maybe she needs to just cry her frustrations out. Let's give it a little time and see if she gives up and falls asleep."

Izzy was surprised that he seemed so unflustered about it, as their child continued to scream bloody murder with no signs of stopping. But maybe he was onto something.

"Just put her in her playpen and see if she goes to sleep. With you holding her, she's getting what she wants, attention."

Izzy didn't know what to think. So, she tried what he suggested. She wrapped Emily snugly in her blanket and laid her gently in the playpen. The cries continued, unabated. Izzy continued to search the internet for answers, and more than once she saw that uncontrolled crying could be a sign of something serious. Twenty minutes went by and Rick looked as frustrated as Izzy felt.

"Why won't she shut up?"

"I don't know. She's never done anything like this before."

"Well, this is pretty miserable." Rick got up and went to the bathroom, then went into the kitchen and opened another beer.

Izzy glared at him. He didn't seem overly concerned that something could be wrong.

"I might as well have another drink. Might make the screaming more bearable."

"Aren't you worried at all?"

"Because she's crying? That's what babies do. Or so they say. I'm not really around them much."

Izzy checked on Emily again, and what she saw alarmed her. Her little face was so red, and she looked so stressed out and miserable. There might be nothing wrong with her, but Izzy wasn't going to just sit around and let her cry any longer. She put her shoes on and put Emily in her carrier. Then slipped on her jacket, found her purse and headed for the door with Emily.

"Where are you going?"

"I'm taking Emily to the ER. This might be nothing, Rick. But it's not normal for her, at all."

He nodded. "Okay, I'll see you when you get back."

"You don't want to come?"

He shook his head. "I have a headache from all that screaming." Izzy did too, but that wasn't the point. She stared at Rick with disappointment.

"Don't look at me like that. I think you're being ridiculous. She's fine. She's just a crier, evidently. Like I said, it's what babies do."

"I'll talk to you later."

Izzy buckled Emily into the backseat of her car and drove off to the ER feeling a mix of emotions. She hoped Rick was right, and that there was nothing wrong with Emily and that she was overreacting. But, when it came to their child, wasn't that a good thing? To make sure nothing was wrong? Rick was certainly no expert on babies. Izzy wasn't either, so she wanted to have Emily seen by someone who was.

She signed into the ER and told them why she was there. They checked Emily's vital signs and then told her to have a seat and they'd call her in shortly. As soon as they sat down, Emily snuggled into her and stopped crying. By the time her name was called, her daughter was sound asleep.

Izzy put her in her carrier and followed the nurse into an examination room. They waited a bit longer and eventually a doctor came in. He was an older man and had a reassuring manner about him. Izzy felt kind of silly now, with Emily sleeping peacefully, but she told him about the incessant crying.

"And this never happened before with her?"

"No, never. She's been a pretty easy baby, so far."

"Okay, let's have a look." The doctor lifted Emily and unwrapped her from the blanket. He laid her on the bed and listened to her heart and checked her vital signs again. Her temperature and everything else was normal.

"Tell me more about tonight. What was different?"

"Well, I'm not married to her father. We've been trying to work things out, and we stayed at his house this weekend for the first time."

"The first time your daughter spent there?"

Izzy nodded. "Yes. First time for both of us since she was born."

"Okay. And do you get along well? Was there any tension between you?"

Izzy thought about that. There definitely was tension, though it was one-sided. Izzy was irritated with Rick's behavior, and he was completely oblivious.

"Maybe a little. Do you think that could be a factor?"

The doctor shrugged. "Hard to say. She's a baby. But if she was in an unfamiliar setting and she sensed that you were upset, then maybe it was all a little too much for her. Possibly just be over-stimulation from too many new experiences. She seems perfectly healthy. There doesn't appear to be anything to be concerned about medically."

"Okay. I'm sorry to have brought her in. My boyfriend told me I was being ridiculous."

"Did he? And you had this conversation in front of the baby?"

Izzy nodded.

"Don't ever feel bad about seeking help for your child. You didn't know, and what if there had been something wrong? You did the right thing by coming in. Now, if I were you, I'd go home, not back to the boyfriend's, and I'd try to get a good night's sleep. Things will be better in the morning."

"Thank you." Izzy felt suddenly lighter, as if a weight had been lifted. She was hugely relieved that Emily was okay and a little annoyed that Rick had been right. Though she thought about what the doctor said and she couldn't help but wonder if Emily picked up on the shift in energy between Izzy and Rick. And if Izzy's irritation with Rick upset Emily. It made sense. Izzy looked at her daughter, who was now sleeping peacefully. The last thing she ever wanted to do was to make her daughter feel afraid or uncomfortable because of a situation that Izzy put her in. She was deep in thought when her phone rang, and it was Rick.

"Hi. We just left the hospital. You were right. She's fine."

"Good. So, I'll see you shortly, then?"

"No. I think I'm going to head home. This has been a long night and Emily's asleep now. I think maybe being in a different setting was part of the problem. I think I just want a good night's sleep in my own bed. I'll call you tomorrow and come by to pick up the playpen."

Rick was quiet for a moment. "You think she was upset because she was at my house?"

"I don't know why she was upset. The doctor said she might have just been confused to be in an unfamiliar environment. Or maybe she just felt like crying. I don't know."

"Right. Babies just cry, like I said earlier. I'll talk to you tomorrow, Izzy."

CHAPTER 26

Izzy woke the next day feeling unusually refreshed. She'd had a good night's sleep and when she checked the time, she was surprised to see that she'd slept until almost eight thirty and she woke to the most wonderful sound—silence.

She slid out of bed and padded into the living room. Mia was on the sofa with Emily sound asleep next to her and Penny keeping a watchful eye on both of them. Penny was in love with Emily and seemed to think she was her personal guard dog. It was cute because Penny was the most non-ferocious dog that Izzy had ever seen.

Mia looked up when Izzy entered the room.

"Good morning. Did you sleep well?"

"I did. Like a log. Thanks for getting up with Emily."

"I figured since you both came back late last night that you could use a few extra hours of sleep. I was in bed early and didn't even hear you guys come in last night. Is everything okay?"

Izzy told her about the night before and the trip to the ER.

"That's interesting. Do you think Emily may have been upset by being at Rick's or that she picked up on any tension between you?"

"It's possible, I don't really know." She sighed. "I have to go over there today and pick up her playpen. And I need to have a conversation I've been putting off for too long. I hoped I wouldn't have to have it."

Izzy saw the sympathy in Mia's eyes and was grateful that she didn't push with any questions. Izzy wasn't ready to talk about what she'd decided she needed to do. She woke up feeling lighter, for the first time in a long time, and sure of what she needed to say to Rick. But it wasn't going to be an easy conversation.

"Why don't you leave Emily here with me. And take as long as you need. I don't have any plans today."

"Thank you." Izzy texted Rick and said she'd be by in an hour to get the playpen. She took a shower and stayed in there longer than she usually did, letting the hot water run over her and delaying the inevitable. She changed and dried her hair, bundled up in layers, turtleneck and a heavy wool sweater, fleece lined jeans and her warmest boots. It was cold out and Izzy hated the cold.

She drove over to Rick's and sat in his driveway for a minute, dreading what she had to do. After a few long moments, she got out of the car and knocked on his front door. He hollered for her to come in and she opened the door. Rick was in his sweats and sitting at the table, drinking coffee. She glanced around the room and noticed the empty beer cans where Rick had been sitting last night. After she left, he had several more drinks. It was the push she needed to start the conversation.

"Rick, we need to talk."

He nodded. "Do you want a coffee?"

"No. I'm good." She sat across from him and took a deep breath. "Rick, this isn't going to work. I hoped that it could. I really did. But it's just not. I'm sorry."

He was quiet, then took a long sip of coffee and stared out the window. He didn't say anything for the longest time, which Izzy eventually found unsettling. She got up finally and went to the playpen and folded it up. When she walked toward the door, Rick finally spoke.

"What is it, really? Is there someone else?"

Izzy turned and looked at him in surprise. "No, of course not. How can you even say that?"

He shrugged. "I don't know what to think, Izzy. Nothing I do is good enough for you. She's my kid, too, you know."

"I know." She thought for a moment, knowing if he fought her in court, he'd be entitled to some kind of custody arrangement. "You could take her one night next weekend, if you like, and we could take it from there. I want to be flexible and work with you on this. But if I do, you have to promise me that you won't drink at all when you're with her. You can't fall asleep on the sofa with her there."

He nodded. "So, it's really over, then? You won't give us another chance?"

She shook her head sadly. "We're just too different,

Rick. But, I hope we can be friends, eventually." She didn't know if he was capable of that. But she hoped he could at least be civil, for their daughter's sake.

"Friends. Okay, Izzy." He spit the words out sarcastically and she wasn't sure how to respond so she stood there, saying nothing. Finally, he sighed dramatically before saying, "I'll call you during the week about taking her one night next weekend."

"Okay. Goodbye, Rick."

He didn't say anything. He just watched her leave. When Izzy reached her car, she put the playpen in the back and drove home, with tears streaming down her face. She really had hoped it would work out. But she'd always worried, deep down, that it wasn't possible. And that became very clear by the way he'd acted over the weekend. If she stayed with Rick, she'd be forever walking on eggshells, waiting for him to unravel, for something to set him off, and she didn't need that in her life. It wasn't fair to her or to her daughter. She really did believe that Emily had picked up on Izzy's tension with Rick and she couldn't put her daughter in that situation again.

Although, she had promised to let Rick take her for a night next weekend, and she hoped that Emily would be okay with that.

When she got home, everyone was in their same

spots as if they hadn't moved since she left. She laughed when she saw it, and then she started to cry. She set the playpen down and leaned against the wall, and the depths of her crying took her by surprise. Everything that she'd been holding in for so long came rushing out. Penny looked alarmed, and Mia jumped up and ran over to her, while Emily continued to sleep soundly. Mia hugged her tight and said nothing, just hugged her and held her close until Izzy finally caught her breath. When they pulled apart, her sister looked at her with sympathy in her eyes.

"So, it's done, then?"

Izzy nodded.

"Do you want some ice cream? I stocked up on chocolate chip the other day."

"My favorite." Izzy scooped herself a big bowl and Mia did the same. They settled in their usual spots and Izzy ate her ice cream and stared out the window. It was a beautiful, sunny day, and she felt both full of hope and so sad at the same time.

"It's almost like a death, when a relationship ends. I feel like I should wear black and go into mourning for a week, at least," she joked.

"It does feel like a death in a way. It's very sad, when you realize what you thought was possible is gone."

"It feels final this time, though. I think I'll be able to move on now. Though there's still visitation with Emily."

Mia frowned. "How will that work?"

"I'm not sure. He said he wants to take her one night next weekend. That's a good start, I suppose. We'll see how it goes. She is his daughter, so I want to be fair to both of them."

"Right. I hope it goes well."

"Me, too."

CHAPTER 27

"I ended things with Rick this weekend, for good."

The news made Will's heart sing and his hopes soar. Izzy announced it matter-of-factly, when the waitress brought their drinks. It was a Tuesday night, and they were at the Rose and Crown for trivia. Mia lifted her glass in a toast.

"Breakups are always sad, but this is a very good thing. I'm glad you did what you felt was best. And now, let's have a great night!"

Will clinked his glass of beer against the glasses of wine and Sam's beer.

"I'm sorry, Izzy. But, I'm happy for you too," he said.

"Thank you. It was a hard weekend, but I definitely feel good about the decision. I'm ready to move on."

They had a fun night and Izzy seemed lighter in mood and laughed more than she had in ages. Luck was with them too, and they came in first place after getting the final question right. That gave them a gift card to use the next time they came for trivia. Mia tucked it in her purse as she was the one that was more organized with things like that.

As they walked to their cars, Will slowed his step and waited until Mia and Sam were out of earshot.

"Which night is Rick taking Emily this weekend?"

"We decided on Saturday night. I'm dropping her off around four."

"Do you have any plans for Saturday night?"

Izzy laughed. "No, no plans. What did you have in mind?"

"Let's go on a date. A real date, me and you, somewhere nice for dinner."

She hesitated, and he worried that it might be too soon, or worse yet that she just didn't think of him that way.

"It's not that big of a deal. It doesn't have to be a date if that feels like too much right now. Maybe it's too soon for you? It could be two good friends going out for a delicious dinner and having a fun night out."

Izzy smiled. "That sounds wonderful, Will. I'd love to."

She didn't say what she was agreeing to other than dinner. Was it a date? Or were they just going as friends? For now, Will was just happy that she said yes. When they reached their cars, he said, "I'll call you on Saturday and we'll make a plan."

"Perfect. Goodnight, Will."

"So, what are you going to wear on your date with Will?" Mia stood in the doorway of Izzy's bedroom and looked amused at the sight of Izzy staring into her closet, trying to decide what to wear. She'd finally lost all of her baby weight and her skinny clothes fit again.

"I don't know what to wear. I'm not sure it really is a date."

"He told you he wanted it to be a date, right?"

"Well, yes. But when I was struck speechless for a moment, just caught off guard, he then said we could just be two friends having dinner, no pressure."

"Well, that sounds good too. What do you want it to be?"

"I like Will. I think I always have. But I wasn't expecting to date anyone so soon after ending things with Rick."

"Well, it has been a long time coming. And Will has been very patient. But if you're not ready to call it a date, just go and have fun. Don't put a label on it."

Izzy relaxed. "Good idea. Now, help me figure out what to wear. The blue sweater or the pink one?" She held up two pretty cashmere sweaters, both long with a flattering v-neck. She'd bought the same sweater in two different colors when she couldn't decide."

"Blue. Looks better with your hair. And I read somewhere that guys always love blue."

Izzy laughed. "Okay, blue it is."

"How was Rick when you dropped Emily off?"

"It was weird, but fine. He was civil, and I felt bad, of course. I showed him again how to heat up her bottle and he assured me that he wouldn't have a drop of alcohol tonight. I reminded him of that, and he promised."

"Good. Don't feel bad, Izzy. You made the right decision. You have to follow your gut. And it's not like you didn't try to make it work."

"I know. You're right."

"Was Emily okay?"

"She seemed to be. She was sleeping when I left."

"Good. Where are you and Will going?"

"The Oak Room at The Whitley."

Mia whistled. "Wow. He's taking you to The Whitley? He's really pulling out all the stops."

"Really? Have you been there? What's it like?"

"I haven't gone there as a customer, but I've been there for wedding tastings with some of my clients. The food is incredible, and the ambience is pure luxury. It's really beautiful."

"Do I need to dress up more? Should I wear a dress?"

Mia shook her head. "It's too cold out for a dress. Wear those dressy black pants you got a while ago. With the flared, wide legs. Those will look perfect with your pale blue sweater."

"Okay. I think I'm a little nervous now."

"Don't be. It's Will. You guys will have a blast."

Izzy finished dressing and getting ready and a little before six, there was a knock on the door. Izzy opened it and her eyes widened. She couldn't remember if she'd ever really seen Will dressed up. He always looked good, but tonight he was in dress pants, a light blue button-down shirt and a deep navy blazer. One she'd never seen before. He was freshly shaved and there was a bit of gel in his hair. His black shoes gleamed as if they'd just been polished. He grinned, and she noticed a dimple pop out in his left cheek. Tonight, Will took her breath away. He smiled and put her at ease, as usual.

"You look gorgeous, Izzy. Though you always do."

She felt herself blush and somewhere deep inside, butterflies took flight. What was happening to her? She'd never had a reaction this strong to Will before.

"You clean up good, Will." Mia came into the living room, followed by Penny, and looked pleased as she saw the two of them standing together. "Have fun, tonight."

The Whitley was on the other side of the island, and it took almost twenty minutes to get there. They chatted easily as they drove, and Will sang along when one of his favorite Jimmy Buffett songs came on the radio. Will had a rich voice and sounded good. How had Izzy never noticed that he could sing, before?

When they reached the Whitley, Will drove down a circular driveway and stopped in front of the valet stand. A tuxedo clad valet driver took Will's keys and wished them both a good dinner.

The lobby of the hotel was impressive. There was white marble everywhere on the walls and floors, and the lobby ceiling was at least thirty feet high. Will led the way to the Oak Room, the hotel's signature restaurant. He gave the hostess his name, and she found the reservation and led them to a lovely table by a window. It was too dark to see anything outside, of course, but the restaurant overlooked the water and Izzy thought that she could hear the ocean ever so faintly in the distance.

"Have you eaten here before?" she asked Will as they opened their menus.

"Yes, once or twice over the years. It was Caroline's favorite restaurant. It's not the kind of place you come to often, though. But it's fun once in a while."

Izzy looked over the menu and everything sounded amazing. When their server came, Will asked if she wanted to share a bottle of wine.

"I'd love to. I didn't know you liked wine?"

"I do now and then. If it's really good wine. Do you like Duckhorn?"

"I've never had it."

"It's one of my favorites. Want to try it?"

"Sure." The server returned a few minutes later with a bottle of a 2017 Duckhorn Cabernet and poured a small amount for Will to try. The color was a rich red and as Will swirled his glass to take a taste, Izzy noticed that it had thick legs that slowly ran down the side of his glass. She wasn't sure what that indicated, but she had a feeling it might be a good thing. Will took a sip and nodded. "It's delicious, thank you." Their server then filled both of their glasses.

"It's good now, but give it a little time to open up and it will be even better."

"Listen to you. I never knew you were so into wine."

"My father was. He used to serve really good ones on holidays and he told us what to look for. I'm more of a beer guy, but now and then I appreciate it with a good meal. And the food here deserves good wine."

Over the next few hours, they enjoyed an incredible dinner. They shared a rich, foie gras appetizer and a table-side Caesar salad for two. They both ordered the house sirloin, which had a coffee rub and was topped with a browned butter and shallot sauce. Whipped potatoes and creamed spinach rounded out the meal. The wine complemented the sirloin perfectly and as Will had said, the wine was wonderful, but after a little while, it opened up and was even smoother and more luscious.

The evening was perfect, but Izzy shouldn't shake an uneasy feeling about Emily. She hoped she'd made the right decision by leaving her with Rick for the night. He was her father, after all, so how could she refuse him? She kept her phone on the table and had told Rick to text or call if he needed anything.

She and Will talked and laughed for several hours. There was never an awkward moment where they ran out of things to talk about. Quite the opposite, as they were both anxious to share all their thoughts and had a lively discussion about everything under the sun. It was a magical night and Izzy was sorry to see it end. Especially when her phone rang as they were halfway home and it was Rick. She could hear Emily in the background, screaming. Izzy instantly tensed up and her heart hurt. She felt bad for both of them. Rick sounded so frazzled and Emily was just distraught and inconsolable.

"Izzy, I'm at my wit's end. I can't get her to stop crying. I've changed her diaper, tried to feed her. I sang to her, held her, left her alone. I don't know what else to do, but she's been crying non-stop now for hours. Can you please come get her?"

"I'll be right there." She turned to Will. "Do you mind swinging by Rick's house? I need to get Emily. She's having a hard night. Rick is too."

"Of course."

Five minutes later, they pulled into Rick's driveway.

"I should probably stay here. I don't want to make things worse. But if you need me, let me know."

"Thanks, Will. I'll be back in a few minutes."

Izzy pulled her winter coat tight around her and knocked on Rick's door. She could hear Emily crying. Rick opened the door. She stepped inside and he handed Emily to her. She clung to Izzy and almost immediately stopped crying.

"Jesus. She just missed her mother. I'm no good at this, Izzy." He looked at Izzy closely and his eyes narrowed. "You look nice. Really nice. Were you on a date?"

Izzy took a deep breath. "I was out to dinner with a good friend."

"Will."

Izzy nodded and then jumped as Rick's fist crashed through the drywall next to the door. He pulled his hand back and his knuckles were bleeding. "Dammit. I knew there had to be someone else. He's had a thing for you for a long time."

"Rick, there wasn't anything going on. This is the first time we've gone out. And I don't know what it is yet."

He stared at her silently for a long moment. "I got laid off yesterday. I didn't do anything wrong this time. My buddy Dave just didn't get that business he was counting on, and he lost another job he thought he was getting this week. He was outbid by Brazilians or maybe it was Jamaicans, I don't remember. But he can't afford to keep me on. He said he might be able to hire me back in a few months, but it's not a definite."

"I'm sorry, Rick." She really did feel for him.

"So, I think I'm going to move off-island for a while. A buddy of mine says there's a ton of work out in Seattle. And the money is good." He looked at Emily and gently pushed her hair off her face. "I just can't be there for her right now. I'm sorry, Izzy. I think this is for the best. I really do. I'll come back when I can, maybe in a year or two. And if things are better then, I can stick around and see if I can be a part of Emily's life maybe."

"Of course. Whatever you want to do, Rick." She held her arms out to him and he pulled her in for a goodbye hug.

Izzy carried Emily and her carrier out to Will's car, and Rick followed with the playpen and Emily's tote bag of diapers and clothes. He put everything in the back seat and then walked back to the house.

"He didn't even look at me," Will said as they drove away.

"He's had a rough couple of days." She told him what happened, and that Rick was leaving.

"Seattle, huh? I heard it's nice out there."

"He said there's a lot of work."

When they reached the condo, Will carried Emily's things in while Izzy brought Emily in her carrier. Mia wasn't home yet. Izzy set Emily down and Will put her things against the living room sofa.

"Well, that was quite a night," Izzy said. "Thank you for a wonderful dinner. And for introducing me to your favorite wine."

Will took her hands and pulled her in close. "It was a good night. The best. Because I was with you. Was this a date for you, Izzy? Or were we just two friends having dinner?" He grinned. "I just want to know."

She smiled. "It was the best date I've ever had."

"Ever?" He looked surprised.

"Ever." And then she pulled him in close and kissed him.

EPILOGUE

"**D**o you think we have enough food? I could put out a few more lobster quiches." Lisa said and then laughed at the expressions on Rhett and Kate's faces.

"Mom, seriously. There's plenty of food. There's always plenty of food. Step out of the kitchen and go enjoy your party." Kate gave her mother a gentle shove and Rhett grabbed her hand and pulled her outside where the sun was shining and her whole family and all of their friends were gathered for a Fourth of July cookout.

Kate was right behind them. "And thank you for having it at your house this year."

"Of course, honey. You have your hands full." She smiled at her daughter who quite literally had her hands full, as Jack handed her babies to her and she balanced one on each side. "Here, I'll take Annabella from you."

Kate handed her granddaughter to her and Lisa walked around showing her off to everyone.

"Who is that with your friend Marley?" Sue asked as she reached for a mini-lobster roll.

Lisa smiled. "That's her client, Mark. He's a photographer. I'm pretty sure they're dating now but she says they are good friends."

"They look cute together," Paige said.

"And are Izzy and Will dating now? They look awfully cute together too. Look at her feeding him a bite of her burger."

"And look how her daughter Emily adores him. She has her little arms wrapped around his neck. You'd almost think she was his daughter," Sue said.

"I think they make a good couple," Lisa said. "They've been friends for a long time."

KATE PLOPPED DOWN NEXT TO JACK, WHO WAS LEANING back on a big blanket that they spread on the lawn. Toby was sleeping next to him and Kate gently laid Annabella next to her brother. They liked to sleep next to each other.

"My mother said Kristen and I used to do that too," she said as Annabella rested her hand on her brother's arm.

"They are too cute. I think we should keep them," Jack said.

Kate leaned over and kissed her husband.

"I agree. They are keepers."

"Are you having fun?"

"Yes. It's been a great day. I love hosting this party but it's a nice treat to just show up and have all the work done, too. It is getting easier, Jack. It's not as overwhelming as it was."

"I think you're doing an amazing job. I still can't believe we have twins. I can't wait until they start walking and talking."

Kate squeezed his hand. "It's going to go by so fast. I don't want to miss a minute. Though I wouldn't mind a few more minutes of sleep."

"Have I mentioned that I love you lately?"

"Actually, I don't believe you have mentioned that today." Kate smiled as Jack pulled her in for another kiss. "Well, I do. I love you, Kate."

———

"I THINK SHE LIKES ME." WILL'S DIMPLE FLASHED AS HE smiled down at Emily and Izzy's heart melted, again.

"I think she loves you, almost as much as her mother does." She said the words first, and the shock on Will's face made her laugh. "You look so surprised."

Will gently untangled Emily from his neck and she yawned as he set her down on the blanket between them and a moment later, she was fast asleep.

"I think I might be having sunstroke. Or did you really just tell me that you love me?"

Izzy beamed up at him happily. They'd been pretty much inseparable since their first date at The Whitley.

"I did, and I do."

"Well, Izzy, you never do fail to surprise me. I think you know I love you too. I have, for a long time, and I'm so glad that we're finally together. I think we're going to have a wonderful future together."

"I know we will."

I HOPE YOU ENJOYED NANTUCKET THREADS! NEXT UP IS A new book in April, called The Hotel, which is The Whitley that you read about in this story.

I'd also like to invite you to join my Pamela Kelley Facebook Reader Group, which is such a fun, happy, feel-good place where we talk about books, pets, food and where I often seek your input on covers, character names, book titles….join the fun today.

Lastly, if you haven't already read it, my most recent release is Christmas at the Restaurant, a sequel to The Restaurant. Both are also set on Nantucket. Thank you!!!